Basketball Fever

...Bring it on!

Basketball Fever

...Bring it on!

HARVEY ERIKSON

ILLUSTRATED BY ROBERT HENRY

MILL CITY PRESS, INC.
212 3ʳᴰ AVENUE NORTH, SUITE 290
MINNEAPOLIS, MN 55401
612.455.2294
WWW.MILLCITYPUBLISHING.COM

ISBN-13: 978-1-62652-583-2
LCCN: 2013902321

COVER ILLUSTRATION BY ROBERT M. HENRY
TYPESET BY JAMES ARNESON

PRINTED IN THE UNITED STATES OF AMERICA

Contents

Preface

December 7, 1941, without warning, the Japanese attacked the U.S. Navy's fleet at Pearl Harbor in Hawaii. It left our nation in a state of shock. Nineteen of our warships were sunk or disabled. Nearly 2,400 servicemen were killed. Our nation plunged into war with Japan. Immediately after the Pearl Harbor attack, Nazi Germany's Adolf Hitler declared war on the U.S. Italy, Germany's partner, followed Germany's lead. As a result, the U.S. found itself fighting two wars at the same time: one on the islands of the Pacific Ocean, and another across the Atlantic Ocean in Europe.

Before the U.S. entered the conflict, the war had been going on for two years and Germany already had conquered most of the countries on the continent of Europe. England and Russia were not yet conquered. This war is called World War Two (WW2). World War One (WWI) was fought twenty-one years earlier. We have been in several wars since WW2, but WW2 was different. It was different because it was a war for our nation's survival!

This is the background for a story about a neat kid - Greg Smith. Despite the terrible war, he is a happy kid with the prospects of a great year in sixth grade coming up soon.

In an instant, however, these dreams are shattered when he learns his father has been drafted. After Father leaves for the Army, Greg and his mother must move from their comfortable surroundings and live with his grandparents in another city.

His worst fears of moving to a new school are realized when he is confronted by the school's uncontested, number one bully. He must use every bit of his quick mind and determination to deal with the large bully's attempts to intimidate and humiliate him.

The reader will get a feeling of what life was like during this horrific war. Wherever our heroic troops were battling was called the "front line." But there was also another "front." This was called the "home front."

The citizens at home had to make sacrifices to support the troops. The very fact that it was given the name "home front" tells of the importance of these sacrifices. This was all-out war and everybody had to pull together to win it. There was not one person in this country who wasn't touched by the war.

We lost over 400,000 of our servicemen. Many were fathers. Countless children said sad good-byes to their fathers in railroad stations all over the country. For many of these children it would be the last time they would see their fathers - ever!

The author of this story was nearly 12 years old when the U.S. entered the war. He grew up living on the "home front" and therefore experienced first hand, life during those trying times. Memories of how he lived and what he saw provide inspiration for many of the scenes in the book.

*This book is dedicated
to all my former students.
You taught me so much!*

Chapter 1

"Clank!" The shaky rim rattled and spit out another shot. But nobody put a butt on him to block out and Greg was able to find a path to the basket. He snatched the ball out of the air and scored. It had been awhile since any of his shots found their way through the hoop.

The weather was hot. Greg was not. It was like the ball was too big for the rim. He hadn't made a shot from over ten feet all afternoon.

The words from his coach kept running through his head: in the art of shooting - don't go left - don't go right - and for *sure* - don't go short! But the scoring recipe wasn't working today. Greg thought, "It's the ball." It was so slick with sweat, it was as if the ball itself was sweating. He just couldn't get a good handle on it.

The game was 3 on 3. Their shirts were thrown aside and pearls of sweat rolled down their tanned bodies. The salty liquid stung when it rolled into Greg's eyes. Finally, exhausted from the heat and exercise, they quit the game. As they split for home one of them hollered a challenge, "Tomorrow, same game, same time, same place."

"You're on," Greg called back and hauled his drained body onto his bike and slowly pedaled toward home. He felt tired, but it was a *good* tiredness. He felt as though he had accomplished something by playing through the sweltering heat and had now earned some do-nothing time.

What a day Greg thought, as he pedaled his way home. Everything, yes, *everything*, was going his way. The summer was coming to an end, but he would be moving into sixth grade with his favorite teacher, Miss Fairchild. She was his teacher in third grade but they shuffled some teachers around and she was assigned to teach sixth grade this year. He liked Miss Fairchild because she was funny and read great stories to her classes. Since there were two classes of sixth grades, he felt fortunate to be placed in her class and not in Miss Frumph's class. Miss Frumph was known as, "Frump the Grump."

But that was only a part of his good luck. Most of his closest friends were going to be in Miss Fairchild's class also. He rolled into the front yard of his home, and with his brakes slipping dangerously, he jumped from the bike. The bike hit the ground with a clatter. He dragged himself up the porch steps, and entered the house. Upon entering the kitchen he was surprised, but pleased, to see his father sitting there. This was at least a good hour before Father's usual return from work. Greg sensed this was not an ordinary kitchen scene. Mother was not cooking dinner. Father didn't usually sit down at the kitchen table after work. Their faces were unsmiling and showed an air of concern. Greg wondered what was behind this gloomy scene. He immediately thought of his ailing Grandfather Smith. Had his sickness worsened? Had he *died*? Greg thought, no, this is not about Grandpa Smith. This is about me! I must have really screwed up. He immediately rewound the last few days in his head trying to figure out what it could be.

Was it the Abigale incident? He didn't really mean to hit his nine year old cousin with that rotten apple. He just wanted to come close, that's all. It sure did splatter that new dress she was wearing. However, the brown color of the rotten apple matched her orange and white dress very well. And those brown splotches of apple gave the dress an entirely new and exiting design. Greg did not share this opinion with his cousin. She was too busy bawling!

The ear splitting wail brought a neighbor out on her porch to determine the cause of the commotion. And the last mistake - he should *never* have run away from the scene of the crime. Would little Abigale somehow forget the name behind this tragedy? Not in her lifetime!

Greg braced himself mentally for what was coming. Better that Grandpa Smith had *died* than this! Immediately, he felt ashamed of this thought and took it back.

His parents looked at each other as if each wanted the other to speak first. Mother broke the silence. "Your father is going to have to leave us." It was one of those statements that come out all in one breath, with nothing leftover for even one more syllable. Tears were welling up in her eyes and Greg turned away. Watching tears come to someone's eyes always brought tears to his own eyes.

"Sit down," his father said. Father quickly broke in to complete the alarming news, "Greg, I've been drafted."

Shocked by this totally unexpected news, Greg blurted out, "But Dad, didn't you say that since you were older, married with a kid, *and* you worked in a defense plant making parts for tanks, you wouldn't be called up for duty?"

Both parents seemed a bit more at ease now that the bad news was out on the table and Father responded, "Well yes, that's what I thought, but rules change when conditions change. Practically the whole world is at war with Germany, Japan, and Italy. Pearl Harbor was a terrible defeat for us and we haven't been doing any better since." Greg was stunned. He just sat there unable to think of one thing to say.

Before he could recover from this awful news, Mother gently took Greg's arm and said, "Greg honey, there's more." *More* Greg thought, how could there be more? But there was. Shaking off her earlier tears she firmly said, "We're going to have to move to Maple City."

"Maple City!" Greg exclaimed, "To Grandma and Grandpa Olson's house?"

"Yes," Mother said. "I know this hurts, but we have no choice."

"There's got to be another way," Greg begged. "There's just *got* to!"

"Look," Mother continued, "there's no way we can afford to live here and make house payments, pay the fuel and electricity bills, the taxes, and make house repairs, on a soldier's pay."

Father said, "Your mother and I have talked all this over. Your mother's mom and dad have that large house and they'd be happy to help us out. They said we could even share their car so that's another expense we could drop. Plus, the Happy Toy Co. is now making war materials. They have expanded their plant and are desperate to find more workers. Your Grandpa Henry said there are 'Help Wanted' signs all over the place."

In a surprised voice Greg asked, "Mom, you'd really work in a factory doing a man's work? *My mother* working in a factory!" The words had a 'How-could-you-do-that!' tone in them.

Father broke in and said, "Greg, lots of women are working in factories now, and doing many other jobs men usually do. There are soldiers on the fighting front, and citizens on the home front. All of us have to pitch in and do our part if we're going to win this war."

Then Mother said in a very determined voice, "Listen to me Son, I can do anything anybody else can do. If other men and women can stand on their feet all day and put pieces of machinery together, I can do that also. If other men and women can put up with the earsplitting noises while working fast and efficiently, I can do that too. I will do it for my family and for my country. Compare working at a factory job, with being on a battlefield fighting and possibly dying for your country. Think about it in that way, Son. By that measure, factory work doesn't seem to be much of a sacrifice at all, does it?"

Greg admired his mother's confidence. And she *was* right. But he could neither look at her, nor say a word, so great was his sorrow at leaving his lifelong home of Riverside, and all his friends he grew up with. As if Mother could read his mind she said, "Greg, having to leave Riverside must be a crushing blow for you. Your father and I realize that. What I have to say to you now is not going to make you feel any better, but it is the truth. First, this is not the greatest disappointment you will have in your lifetime, although it might seem like it now. Second, you have all the courage inside you, to make this move a good one. Look for it. And last, think about the one person in our family who is making the greatest sacrifice. We are all in this together - like a team. And for certain, we *can* do it!"

Greg agreed with all those reasonable words. They were words of true inspiration. But at this particular point in his life there were no words that could lift this blanket of despair that was smothering him. He arose from his chair and quietly said, "I think I'll go to my room now." He knew he should say more. He knew he should say something that would indicate he understood the problem. He should tell them not to worry, and that he will be okay. The urge to do so was there. The breath to give those words life was not. He went to his room.

He entered his room and belly flopped on his bed. He kept up on the war by occasionally reading the paper. He knew things were not going well and even went so far as to wonder what it would be like if we lost the war. He could not imagine Hitler of Germany, Mussolini of Italy, or Emperor Hirohito of Japan, actually ruling the United States. Would the crooked-crossed Nazi flag fly over our U.S. Capitol in Washington, D.C.?

His thoughts of war were quickly shoved aside as he lie there trying to digest all the bad news of the day. He made a mental list of all the great things he would have to leave behind: his friends, his school, his teacher Miss Fairchild, his basketball team, this room he loved, but most of all - Father. And then, the worst of all thoughts surfaced in his mind. Would his father ever return? As he closed his eyes, tears squeezed out onto his pillowcase.

It wasn't very long before Father had to leave. The parting at the train station was not easy. Greg knew he would always remember every detail of the scene. Father was as usual, upbeat and cheerful. He reminded Greg that he should work to help his elderly grandparents as much as possible. He said once more, that it was a very fine thing Grandmother and Grandfather Olson were doing for them.

The train finally appeared, and with much hissing of steam and clanking of iron, ground to a screeching halt. Mother and Father embraced. Then Father turned to Greg, and ruffling his hair said, "Goodbye little buddy. Take good care of yourself and study hard." Father then boarded the train, turned and waved to them, and disappeared into the passenger car. Greg and his mother, Rose, hurried along side the train, peering through the windows, trying to get one last look at Father. They could not. With a violent jerk, the huge metal monster slowly began to chug away. And so it was that William "Will" Smith left his home and loved ones to defend his country just as thousands of other young men from all over the country were doing. Father was gone. Greg immediately felt the loss. It was as if there was some great hole opening up in his life, like a kind of vacuum.

On the way home Mother was keenly aware of Greg's sorrow. She said, "It's a sad time, isn't it. But Greg, we have a choice. We can mope around and complain, and feel sorry for ourselves, or we can look forward. Nobody ever forgets the past, but everybody on this earth has a future. And it's the future that we need to be thinking of right now. That is what your dad wants and expects of us. We can't let him down. Let's finish up what we have to do here in Riverside and move on." He wanted to support Mother and say the right thing. He truly did. But the words would not come out. He turned his head, stared blankly out the window, and fought back tears.

Chapter 2

Getting ready to move was a big job. Since they were moving into a house that was already filled with stuff, Mother had to give away or sell all their furniture, appliances, and other household items. But these tasks were finally settled, goodbyes were said, and the house was put up for sale by a realtor who was a good friend of the family. The "FOR SALE" sign that was put up in their front yard seemed out of place. Greg had seen many of them before, but he never once thought he would see one in *his* yard.

Their 1937 4-door Hudson was jam-packed with clothes and personal items. "Well," Mother said as she started the car, "take a last look at the place and store it in your memory box. It might be a long time before you see it again." Halfway out of the drive she stopped the car and said to Greg, "Look in the glove compartment and get the camera, would you please?" She got out of the car and snapped three pictures of the cute little bungalow with the tidy front lawn. "I hope someone enjoys our old home as much as we did," she said.

They had visited Grandma and Grandpa's home several times over the years. They were Henry and Henrietta Olson. They lived in an old white square, two-story home. The home had that solid look to it, like it was ready for anything. They were good grandparents but very particular about their home. More than once,

Greg remembered Grandpa Henry telling him, "We've got a place for everything, and everything in its place. Yes siree young man, remember that and life will be a lot easier for you. That's the way it was when I was in the submarine service during the Great War. There wasn't much room in the sub, so we had to have a place for everything, and everything in its place. Yep, close quarters. I slept atop a torpedo! A place for everything and everything in its place. Remember that Son. Works in this house too."

Both Grandma and Grandpa were hard of hearing and spoke louder than was necessary. Grandpa claimed three years in the submarine service, with all that din and clattering, started the loss of his hearing. One time Greg asked, "If submarines are so loud, how come they call it the 'silent service'?"

"Well Son, that's a good question," Grandpa answered. "You see a submarine runs pretty quiet on the outside. But on the inside there is the din of those ear shattering, battery-powered engines. But let me tell you this, whenever there was an enemy ship above us, throwing depth charges down at us, we'd shut off those engines and just sit there. None of us moved. An enemy sailor would be sitting up there in some big ol' destroyer. He'd wear earphones hooked up to very sensitive equipment that would pick up any underwater noise. We'd be a hidin' *down* there. They'd be a listenin' *up* there. Then pretty soon those depth charges would go off. Boom! Boom! If they got close, the explosives would rock the boat. Sometimes the blast would cause leaks and we'd have water pouring in. Some excitement then, let me tell you!"

Then as always, he would roll up the sleeve of his right arm and point to his old, faded tattoo. It showed two dolphins on either side of a sub coming straight at you. Greg thought that was neat. He always liked Grandpa's war stories, but if Grandma was around she would be quick to interrupt. She would say, "Greg's probably tired of hearing your old war stories. Why don't you ask him what *he's* been doing?" Greg always thought that was kind of a put-down, but Grandpa never seemed to mind. He would just get up and say that it's about time for him to get on with some chore or repair he had to make.

After several hours of driving, they turned into his grandparents' driveway. Brightly colored flowers were growing around the foundation of a large screened- in front porch. A swing hung from the ceiling of the porch where Grandma and Grandpa were sitting. Mother and Greg got out of the car, stretched, and walked to greet them. After the warm greetings, Greg knew exactly what was coming next. It was a common statement every kid has heard. Grandma Henrietta put her hands on her hips, stepped back, looked Greg up and down and exclaimed, "My, how you have grown!" She said it as all grandmothers do, with some surprise and admiration. Greg never liked that much attention and was glad when it was over. He never knew how to respond, but he had given it some thought this time and was ready.

"Well thank you," Greg said sincerely. "But you know Grandma, growing is what I'm *supposed* to do. Much better than *shrinking*, don't you think?"

Grandma looked somewhat puzzled for a moment. The pause made Greg wonder whether he had stepped over the boundary between humor and good manners. But Grandma Henrietta took the reply in good spirits. "People don't shrink smarty pants. If that were true we'd just disappear after awhile."

Grandpa Henry said, "Why don't you and your mother follow me upstairs and I'll show you to your new quarters." They trudged up the long open stairway holding onto the finely polished banister. Mother was to occupy the largest of the two bedrooms and Greg the smaller one across the hall. Unlike Mother's room which was furnished, this room was empty. Grandpa said, "After dinner you can help me drag down a bed and a dresser from the attic. There's a card table and a desk lamp up there also. You can use that as a study table."

Greg looked the room over. It was small compared to the other rooms in the house, but it had a window twice the size a regular window. Plus, a maple tree had grown rather close to the house that made it seem like you were in a tree house. Yes, he thought, this is not bad at all.

Greg brought in his stuff from the car. He threw the sack of clothes into the room. There was an echo as the sack hit the floor and clothes spilled out on the bare boards of the floor. He always liked empty rooms and the way echoes danced between the walls. But not this time. Worries haunted him: a new city, a new home, a new school, new friends. How would all this play out? Mother's inspiring words about the move were fading fast. Yes, he had visited his grandparents' home before, but only for short stays. This time it was for the duration of the war. And who only knows how long that would be. In a few days school was to start. Whatever would that be like he wondered?

Mother peeked in the room and asked, "How you doing kid?"

"Terrible!" Greg moaned.

Seeing his clothes scattered about the floor, Mother scolded, "Greg, those clothes are clean and ironed. If you are going to mistreat them you can start doing your own laundry." Greg was going into sixth grade. Too young to worry about doing his laundry, he thought. Bending over he slowly picked up his clothes. He put them back in the sack and listlessly dragged himself over to the doorway.

"They will tease me," Greg complained.

"Who will tease you?" Mother asked.

"All the kids in my new school, that's who. We got a new kid in our class last year and just about everybody teased him."

"Did you join in on the teasing?" Mother questioned. Greg did not answer, but he remembered how he also took his turn at teasing the new boy. He went so far as to "accidentally" knock the boys cap off at recess. The cap landed in a puddle of water. Several older boys standing nearby smiled as the new kid fished it out of the puddle, and slowly emptied the water out of the hat. It was not something he would usually do and immediately he felt guilty about it. Still, he accepted the older boys' praise and attention, by smiling back at them.

Grandpa Henry and Greg carried a few sticks of furniture and a bed and mattress from the attic, dusted them off, and placed them in the room. Grandpa produced fresh linens and Greg made his bed. He folded his clothes and placed them in the old dresser also brought from the attic. The drawers stuck, but Grandpa said he would slicken them up with some beeswax.

The awful thought of going to a new school continued to simmer in the back of his mind. He kept thinking, "What if *this* would happen?" or "What if *that* would happen?" He would fill in the unanswered questions with all sorts of embarrassing and disastrous calamities. Greg had a lively imagination and it was now out of control in a negative way.

After dinner and much catch-up conversation, he said goodnight and went upstairs to bed. Before drifting off to a fitful sleep, he wondered where his father was sleeping tonight.

Chapter 3

After a few short days and many worries, it was time for Greg to dive into the new school year. The alarm jarred him out of his sleep. Monday morning rolled around too fast. He turned the jangling alarm off, fluffed up his pillow, closed his eyes, and said goodbye to the morning. Not two minutes went by before he felt someone shaking his leg.

"C'mon Son, up and at 'em. Big day for you," Mother said encouragingly. Greg just hated to see anybody that cheerful, when *he* felt so grumpy.

"I'm getting up, I'm getting up. I need just five more minutes," Greg pleaded.

"Not a chance," Mother ordered. "It's time for you to crank up that motor of yours and get going!"

Breakfast brought much of the same disgustingly cheerful chatter. One uplifting phrase after another rolled off her busy tongue: "It won't be so bad. You'll make friends. You can do it." And so it went, on and on. All Greg wanted to do is to go back to the safety of his room and sleep. He thought he could spend the remainder of his life in that room. Anything would be better than coming face to face with all those new kids.

The walk to his new school seemed to take forever. A group of kids were walking ahead of him. They were walking at a pace slower than a snoozing snail. But there was no way he was going to pass them and invite some "friendly" conversation. So he lagged back and hoped they would at least get to school on time. They did and he did.

As he walked onto the crowded playground, he was certain he caught several kids staring at him. He thought he saw a girl point to him, and then cupping her hand over her mouth, lean toward a friend and say something. It was probably, "Look at the new kid," or something worse. He felt like a spotlight was on him and he hated that. He walked over to the building near the doorway and leaned against the wall. At least nobody could sneak up behind him. He got rather comfortable there. Maybe Mother was right, this wasn't so bad after all. He imagined himself enjoying the scene. In a few minutes the bell rang and it was time to go in.

The teacher was Miss Johnson, a tall, lean, young woman. Since this was the first day of school everyone was a bit confused as to where to sit. It even appeared to Greg that some of the kids looked as lost as he *felt.* The desks were all fastened together in rows front to back, a solid line, and immoveable. Each one touched the other, and were bolted to the floor. It gave him a locked-in feeling. No sliding these desks around like in his old school.

Greg thought he was lucky to find an empty desk in the far corner of the room. At least he wouldn't be "on display" in front of the class. Miss Johnson welcomed the students to the sixth grade and called the roll. Everyone who was supposed to be there, was there. Then she began reading the school rules to the class. She added many extra details to the rules and Greg thought this was boring. But that was okay because all he had to do was just sit there. Also, time was moving on and it was as if nobody knew he existed. Maybe Mom was right, so far so good, no problems.

Greg took a little side trip from the goings on in the class. He often did this in school. Of course this wasn't the usual type of trip where you actually *go* somewhere. This trip was all in his head. His mind was like a radio. If you get tired of listening to one station, you turn the dial and get another station. He often dreamed about his favorite sport - basketball. Just wait till these guys see what I can do with a basketball. He pictured himself making one shot after another. A radio announcer would say, "And Smith scores *again*. Wow, what a great shot!"

Greg's daydreams were interrupted when a man stepped through the door. It was the principal, Percy Picklehoffer, and he gave the students a friendly welcome. He was a small man but had a very deep voice. He wore round, gold rimmed glasses, and had a moustache. He went over some of the same school rules he had heard from Miss Johnson. But he left before Greg could slip into another one of his all-in-the-mind basketball games.

Chapter 4

After Mr. Picklehoffer left, Miss Johnson announced it was time to pass out the textbooks. Hands shot up in the air of all those volunteering to pass them out. Greg's hand was not one of those. *He* was not going to volunteer for anything! He felt safe right where he was, and he was determined to stay put.

Miss Johnson chose the first person in each row for the task. Then, there was a flurry of activity as books were counted and each student started down the row with his or her pile of books.

The boy passing out books in Greg's row was big for a sixth grader, in both weight and height. He had a wide grin that showed big white teeth. He seemed to know everyone. Greg thought he was not the type of person to choose a front row seat. But then he remembered Miss Johnson escorting him to that desk, looking him straight in the eye, and pointing to that seat. Though no words were said, it was obvious it was a command not a request. The large boy had gotten into a shoving match with somebody in the coat hall. It was all good natured and not serious, but Miss Johnson was having none of it.

When he got to Greg's desk he had one book left in his hand. He gave Greg his great big smile. Greg smiled back. He offered the book to Greg, but before Greg could touch it, the boy dropped the book. It landed on the floor with a loud smack. The boy kept the smile on his face, looked straight at Greg and said, "Oops!"

Greg knew it was no accident and felt a swell of emotions race through him. First it was fear, and then it turned to anger.

And here suddenly was the next set of books being flipped out on each desk by this huge lad: social studies books this time. Thoughts swirled around in Greg's mind. How would this overgrown vandal deliver his book this time? He still carried that wide grin and joked with the students as he passed them out. When he got to the person sitting directly in front of Greg, he stopped and laid the book very carefully on top of the first one. He took his time to make sure the corners and edges of the books were perfectly in line. How nice and neat! Greg was next and bursting with curiosity. How would the brute deliver his book *this* time?

He took two measured steps toward Greg's desk. The large fellow smiled down at Greg again. Greg folded his arms across his chest and leaned back in his desk. He then looked away from the boy who was holding the book, and out the window as if nobody was there. He could see out of the corner of his eye that the book was being held only about a foot from his desk. Should he take it? Maybe the kid was just fooling around before and really wants him to take it this time.

Should he forgive, forget, and take it, he wondered? All this time the boy with the book just stood there, like a statue. The book was in his hand and he was patiently waiting for Greg to make his move.

Greg made his decision. He quickly reached for the book. Too late! The large lad dropped it to the floor with the other one.

"Rocco," Miss Johnson said, "if you want to keep your job you're going to have to speed up your deliveries."

After this warning Rocco hurried to the front of the room like he was on a very important mission. In a very business-like manner he promptly passed out the books to everyone in the row. However, he stopped when he got to Greg's desk. Again he held out the book for Greg to take. As fast as he could, Greg grabbed for the book.

Not fast enough. Rocco jerked it away. Then he offered it back to Greg. Greg grabbed. Rocco jerked. Greg grabbed. Rocco jerked. Rocco took a quick glance back over is shoulder to find Miss Johnson attending to other matters. Rocco then slipped the book to the floor. The students sitting near him were smiling at each other at this teasing, but not wanting to laugh out loud. Other books were delivered in variously creative ways, all landing on the floor. Greg now was more amused at this, than angered. Besides, he had a plan. He bent over and stacked all the books up in a single pile.

There was one more book to be passed out. Rocco seemed to be tiring of the job now. He said nothing to the students and walked briskly. Greg had raised his desk lid so there was no place to put the book but on the floor. Rocco put the book on top of the mounting stack of books under the desk.

As soon as Rocco turned his back to leave, Greg gave the stack of books a swift kick. The books sailed across the aisle like a spilled deck of fresh playing cards. The clatter pierced the silence of the room. Miss Johnson had been writing some assignments on the board and had not noticed Rocco's sneaky little tricks. When the books hit the floor, every member of the class turned around to see what caused the noise. So did Miss Johnson.

"What's going on back there?" she asked. Greg just sat there with his arms folded looking out the window. Let Rocco answer that one, he thought. He's the one who started it all.

Then she asked, "Whose books are those scattered all over the floor?" Greg figured that was one *he* should answer. After all, they *were* his books.

"They're mine," he responded.

"Maybe you could tell me why they are on the floor," she demanded.

"Because, Miss Johnson, that is where your *passer-outer* put them," he replied. The class laughed at the term *passer-outer.* This displeased her even more. She scowled at Rocco. "Rocco," she said firmly, "Did you put those books on the floor?"

He looked back at the books strewn on the floor, and with a voice that sounded more like a holler said, "No!"

"Yes he did! Yes he did!" three girls in a chorus shouted. "We all saw him, Miss Johnson."

"Okay, well I did. But not like that." He gestured to the books with his outstretched hand. "Not all over the floor."

Then one of the girls said, "The stack of books got so high they probably just fell over."

Greg knew she saw him give the pile a kick and appreciated her backup. Rocco gave her a dirty look and said scornfully, "Yeah, fell over my foot!"

One of the girls giggled and whispered to another, "Not *your* foot, the new kid's foot!"

Miss Johnson looked at Greg and asked, "Did you kick the pile of books over?"

He answered, "I guess I might have given them an accidental nudge. Wasn't much room down there for my feet."

Miss Johnson gave Greg a suspicious look but asked no further questions.

Her guess was an intentional "kick" but dealing with Rocco was first on her mind.

Miss Johnson walked over to Rocco, who with elbows on desk, was leaning on both hands. He was staring ahead at nothing. She bent over, and putting her hands on her knees, looked intently into Rocco's face. There was no smile on her face. She said, "Since this is not the first of your little tricks this morning, I think you and I should have a serious talk at recess. Now, I think it would be a very nice thing if you went back there and picked up those books, set them back on his desk, and tell our new student that you are sorry."

Rocco's head turned toward the ceiling and he took a deep breath. When he expelled the breath it sounded like a hiss. The class quietly watched as he trudged to the back of the room. He stacked the books all in one pile, picked the whole thing up, and took the few steps to Greg's desk. Then he stopped, but made no effort to put them down. He just stood there and glared at Greg. He held the books about a foot over the desk, then dropped them. They hit the desk with a thud, shattering the silence of the room. Then, in a voice that could be heard two rooms away, Rocco said, "SORRY!" It was the most *un- sorriest* "sorry" anyone could ever imagine. Miss Johnson noticed, but decided to deal with it during recess.

Chapter 5

Greg felt good about how everything turned out. He knew, however, he would have to pay for this good feeling later. Rocco will want payback. He hoped Miss Johnson would keep Rocco in his cage for the entire recess. Turn him loose earlier, and it would mean big trouble. Greg was certain of this. A picture of Rocco challenging him on the playground kept floating around in his head. It was a little over an hour until recess. It was one of those rare times he wanted the hands of a school clock to slow down.

The shrill sound of the bell jarred him to the fact that he must now set his feet on the playground. Miss Johnson dismissed the class by rows. As he left, Greg looked over his shoulder to see if his enemy was still in his seat. He was. The playground was a busy place. Not knowing anyone made him feel like a guest who was just passing through. But a second thought told him this was his school home now, and he'd just have to get used to it.

"Want to play catch?" a voice from behind him asked. He turned around to see a boy who looked like himself. He had the same brown hair, medium size, and had the same type of flat nose, like a bulldog. He always hated his nose because it just seemed to be a dot in the middle of his face. It was as if it was made of putty and he ran into a wall. Worse, one time in third grade, a girl called it a "cute little button nose."

The boy broke into Greg's thoughts by asking him a second time, "Want to play some catch with me?"

"Sure, why not," Greg replied.

"My name is Fred, but everybody calls me Poker. One time, Rocco, you know, the guy you got into it with today, well, he just called me that name one day, and it stuck. Rocco's got a way with names. If he calls you a name you're stuck with it. You own it man. You might as well paste it on your forehead. I don't mind the name though. I really kind of like it. You're Greg, right?"

"You got it," Greg answered.

Poker said, "Rocco'll have a name for you I'll bet." Then he laughed and said, "Probably won't be anything you'll be proud to wear, after what happened today. Rocco's like an elephant in a couple of ways. He never forgets, and he's as strong as one."

They threw a football back and forth a few times before the boy asked, "Where'd you move in from?"

"Riverside. Ever heard of it?"

"Sure," the boy replied. "They play some good basketball over there. Seems like they're always in the state tournament."

Greg felt good to know people around the state knew about Riverside being a basketball power. "Yep," he answered. "And they'll be good this year too because they got a lot of experienced players coming back."

"That was pretty cool what you did to Rocco today, you know, kicking over that pile of books," Poker said.

Greg didn't want to make a big deal out of it, so he just shrugged his shoulders and said nothing. The boy went on, "He's probably catching it from Miss Johnson right now." He smiled as though the thought of Miss Johnson lecturing Rocco gave him some pleasure. Despite the fact that Greg didn't want any credit for what he did, he felt good about what the boy said. Didn't every kid want to be "cool" he thought? However, any good feelings he got from what Poker said, was quickly overcome by what he said next.

"Do you know what Rocco's last name is?" Poker asked. Before Greg could respond the boy said, "It's Hardknuckle, yeah, Rocco Hardknuckle. Ever heard of a name like that? Sometimes they call him "The Rock." Good name for him too, because he's tough. There's not a kid in the whole school who would mess with him. Not since fourth grade when he took on a sixth grader called Big Mike. Mike even flunked once so he should have been in *seventh* grade. Didn't bother Rocco. He hit Big Mike three times before anybody knew what happened. Gee! Mike went down on one knee and he even cried a little bit. I didn't blame him though. He lost a tooth and his mouth was all bloody." Their game of catch was not very lively by this time. It was more of an excuse to talk.

"Well, I gotta run now," the boy said. As he turned to leave he shouted back over his shoulder, "If I see Rocco coming out, I'll try and let you know."

"Thanks." Greg said. Thanks for *what* he thought, for telling me what a big hole I've dug for myself? Here I am, the first day in a new school, and I make an enemy of the toughest guy in school. How could your first day in a new school go any worse than that? He wished the bell would ring. He stood with his back to the wall, but in a position where he could keep an eye on the door. If Rocco showed his face, he wanted to see it. However, if it happened, he still didn't have a clue as to what he would do. He went over his options. He could run. That was no good because he would be called a coward. He could try and talk himself out of it. That probably wouldn't work with Rocco. Rocco would want to hit him first, and then talk. He could fight. That wouldn't work because he couldn't beat Rocco with the help of a baseball bat. An apology? That would be like running away also. Besides, Rocco started this whole thing and he *wasn't* sorry. He could tell the teacher but that would mean he needed help to deal with his own problems. And, he'd be a tattletale. Besides, the teacher couldn't be with him all the time. She wasn't paid to be a bodyguard. Greg did not like any of his options. He would just have to wait and make the decision about what to do, when and if something happened. Before he had time to think anymore about it, the bell sounded and all the kids ran to line up. There was a lot of shoving and several kids cut in front of him. He didn't like that but he didn't say anything either. He figured he had gotten himself into enough trouble today without asking for more.

As he entered the room he could hardly wait to see what Rocco was doing. Miss Johnson was greeting the kids at the door. On the bulletin board in the back of the room was spelled out in big letters, "WELCOME TO SIXTH GRADE." Earlier in the morning, each student had written their names on bright yellow tags made of poster paper. Rocco had an ugly frown on his face as he tacked them up. Greg smiled as he viewed the scene. Rocco was unusually silent, and avoided looking at the other students as they came in. A good friend of Rocco's by the name of Scott came over to where Rocco was working. He put his hands on his hips and looked up and down at the bulletin board. He then turned to Rocco, and with pretended enthusiasm, nodded and said, "Gee Rocco, NICE WORK!"

Rocco didn't look at Scott but growled, "Yeah, and you'd look good with a row of these tacks in your forehead, you know, Frankenstein-like."

Miss Johnson began the class by pointing out the bulletin board which Rocco was just now finishing. She said in a very lively voice, "Rocco here was nice enough to help me put up this display during recess. Didn't he do a good job?" There were quite a few smiles over this statement. Everybody knew why Rocco helped with the display, and it wasn't because he was an eager volunteer. Upon hearing his name, Rocco, now seated, slumped down even further in his desk in a futile attempt to disappear.

Miss Johnson continued, "We have some new students in class this year and I want each of you to do all you can to make them feel at home. Treat them as you would like to be treated if *you* moved to a new school." And then Miss Johnson asked, "How many of you have moved to a new school at some point in your life?" Greg was surprised at how many students raised their hands. Miss Johnson even raised her hand.

He wondered how many of them had as bad a time as he was having? Not a one! He would bet anything on that. He knew that at recess he was just lucky because Rocco was caged up in the room. He would not be so lucky at lunch time. Again, dreading the arrival of lunch time, he wanted the hands on the clock to slow down.

He wondered why every time he wanted the hands of a clock to slow down, they always seemed to go faster. And every time he wanted them to go faster, they always slowed down. And so the rest of the morning raced by. The bell rang. The rows of students were dismissed one at a time. He didn't have any idea where the lunch-room was, but he would just follow the other kids. Each student grabbed their sack lunch as they passed through the coat hall. Greg felt a hollow pain in his stomach and he didn't know whether it was hunger or if he was homesick for his old school.

He wanted to stay well behind Rocco in the line. As they walked through the hall in a loose sort of line, Greg made sure he stayed toward the back. He didn't have to worry, however, because Rocco was setting a good pace, half walking, half running. He had passed several others and now headed the line. They went to the gym to eat their lunch where tables had been set up. As they entered the gym, a large woman with a clipboard in her hand awaited the pupils. "Please take a seat promptly," she ordered. Rocco seated himself with some other loud and boisterous students. The entire table where Rocco was sitting was noisy. She walked over behind Rocco, and put her hands on his shoulders. She said nothing, but simply looked at the students. They all got quiet. She didn't look like the type of person who would put up with any rowdy behavior. The principal came in. In his deep voice he began to tell them about the rules. He spoke slowly and seemed to measure each word. He told them he hoped everybody would have a good year and learn lots of interesting things. He said that excitement is bad for the digestion, so we should all behave during lunch. Those who cannot behave will have to eat in his office, alone, and in silence. Greg thought Mr. Picklehoffer sounded strict. For now at least, he was glad about that.

On the playground, Greg found his spot by the building where he stood earlier during recess. He leaned his back against the sun-warmed bricks of the old building. He could view the entire playground and it was important to keep an eye on Rocco. He also wanted to know where the teacher on duty was, just in case. He had decided not to tell the teacher about his problem with Rocco. Nevertheless, it wouldn't hurt to know where he could get help if he really needed it.

Shortly, Poker, the boy he had met at recess came over, "Want to play some catch again?" he asked. Greg was not really interested, but he looked around to see where Rocco was. He was on the other side of the playground teasing some girls. The scene looked safe enough to play a short game of catch.

"Sure, why not," Greg answered.

Poker said, "I couldn't get the football this time. This kickball was all that was left." Greg thought it was kind of dumb to play catch with a kickball but he went along with it. The boy made a wild throw that Greg had to run for to make the catch.

Greg said, "We'll pretend it's a football. Go out for a pass." Poker ran and Greg passed it to him. Poker made a nice catch. "Hey, great catch, Poker," Greg hollered. Without a word to Greg, Poker turned his back and walked away, bouncing the ball in front of him. That's strange Greg thought. Why would he leave so suddenly?

Chapter 6

In the next instant, Greg felt a hard slap on his back. The slap landed on his shoulder blade, where friendly slaps often land. But this slap was too hard to be friendly. It hurt! The force of it caused Greg to take a couple of steps forward to keep from losing his balance. Before he could turn around, he was locked in a one-armed bear hug. He felt his feet slowly leave the ground. His body stopped rising after it was suspended a few inches off the playground. A voice not two inches from his ear said, "Well, if it ain't my little buddy. I've sort of been looking around for you."

Greg did not need to turn his head to see who it was. But he did. As suspected, he found himself eye-to-eye with Rocco. Greg was caught completely off guard, his feet still dangling in mid-air. Rocco grinned widely and said, "You know I can really squeeze hard when I use two arms. Like maybe your eyeballs pop out of their sockets and roll on the ground with the ants." Rocco loosened his grip and Greg's feet finally found the ground. Rocco said, "But I only used one arm this time because Teach said we should be nice to you new guys. I don't really buy that stuff but I don't want to be locked up for recess anymore either. Just know that someday you're going to have to pay for knocking those books over and getting me in trouble."

The whole scene could have ended right there with Rocco's last statement. But Greg could not let the warning pass by him without an answer. As Rocco began to walk away, Greg shot back, "It wasn't me who stacked the books on the floor. Why should I pick them up?"

The words flew out of Greg's mouth before he had time to think of the consequences. Once they were out of his mouth and airborn, there was no getting them back.

Rocco turned to some boys who were with him and gestured with his arms out. "Nice guy huh! Let him off easy and he turns into a smart mouth."

"Let me off!" Greg snapped. "You were giving me a hard time and you know it. What if I delivered *your* books on the floor? I'd be carrying my teeth home in my lunch sack." Then Greg allowed a slight smile to break over his face and said, "Besides, it looked like you were having lots of fun working on the teacher's bulletin board." As he finished this remark, he turned and quickly began to walk away. Then Greg looked back over his shoulder and said, "Just kidding big guy. Don't be going all hyper."

The three boys who were with Rocco, picked up on Greg's teasing comment. One said, "Yeah, it looked like you were having a real ball sticking all those tacks in the board."

Another laughed and said, "Sure beats going out for recess doesn't it?"

Rocco put up his fists like he was going to fight. He cracked a smile and gave one of them a tap on the arm, not too lightly. "More for you later," he warned.

As Greg looked at all that happened, he was glad to know that Rocco could take some kidding, at least from his friends. He was a good distance away now scuffling with yet another student. For now, he seemed to have lost interest in challenging Greg. He had found other prey to tease and muscle around.

The bell rang and the kids ran to get in line. The rest of the afternoon went fast because they had so much work to do. During gym class Rocco and Greg were on the same kickball team but Rocco ignored him and Greg was happy about that.

The few minutes before dismissal were different. Rocco looked to the back of the row several times as though he wanted to make sure Greg was still there. "Please finish the assignment," Miss Johnson urged. "If you are having trouble with it, I can help you after school. In fact, if you do not have it done please stay until you do. With a little help from me, I'm sure it won't take you long."

Greg could tell right away who did not have it done because their heads snapped back to look at the clock almost as one. Rocco's head, however, didn't exactly snap. It just did a slow roll back over his shoulder in that direction. He squinted at the clock for a couple of seconds, turned back around, and carelessly threw his pencil down on his desk. He then slumped back into his half-sitting, half-lying position. It was obvious to Greg that Rocco had given up on the assignment. Rocco would be staying after school and he, Greg, would have a pleasant, carefree walk home. He breathed a long sigh of relief!

"Would the last person in the row please collect the papers?" Miss Johnson asked. Greg was the last one in the row and began collecting the papers. When he got to Rocco's desk, Greg waited for the paper or some response. Nothing. Rocco looked away. Greg assumed he did not have the assignment done and walked away. He walked two steps past Rocco's desk and was tripped. Greg did not turn around to see who did it. He already knew.

Chapter 7

While walking home he thought about his first day in his new school. Everything went fine except for Rocco. He liked his teacher, Miss Johnson. The kids seemed decent. He was able to get all his work done. But what would he do about Rocco?

No sooner had he entered the house, Mother asked, "Well I see you survived."

"Yes I did," he answered. Greg didn't know what else to say. Should he tell his mother that he had made an enemy of the toughest sixth grader on the planet? Should he tell her that this overgrown brute promised to get him? Should he tell Mother the whole story: the books on the floor, being lifted off the playground with one arm, the possibility of his eyeballs rolling on the ground with the ants, the tripping incident? He expected his mother to ask him to tell her about his day. But that didn't happen. Mother asked him to do a few chores and reminded him to get his homework done. She asked nothing about the details of the day. Good, he thought, that would give him more time to think about what to say.

By dinnertime he had decided to say nothing about his problem. When asked, he said he liked his teacher, his principal seemed strict, and he got his work done. Mother asked, "Did you make any friends?"

Greg simply replied, "No." Mother asked nothing more and Greg told no more. He would see if he could handle the "Rocco Hardknuckle problem" on his own.

When Mother was done eating she said, "I think I'll drink my coffee out on the porch." Grandpa Henry began another submarine story about when there was some kind of mechanical failure and they couldn't get the sub to surface. Greg was excited to hear about it, but Grandma was not.

Grandma Henrietta said, "Why don't you ask Greg what *he's* been doing?"

Grandpa Henry strained to hear the question and replied, "Why would he be moving? He just got here."

"Okay," Grandma said, "Just ask him, will you?"

Grandpa Henry looked puzzled and asked, "Greg, are you moving?"

Greg, who had been following this communication mix-up attempted to straighten things out. He said clearly and slowly, "Grandma said to ask me what I was *doing*, not if I was *moving.*"

"Losing what?" Grandpa asked. "Just let me know, because I can find anything around here. Yes siree young man, a place for everything and everything in its place."

Again, Greg explained patiently, "I didn't *lose* anything. Grandma said to ask me what I was *doing.*"

Grandma said, "Your grandpa's right Son, if you've lost any-thing he can sure find it. What was it you lost?"

At this point, Greg totally gave up and replied, "Nothing. I'm going to get my basketball and shoot a few baskets."

Grandpa Henry said, "I think I'll go down the basement and work."

Grandma Henrietta said, "I wouldn't look in the basement, Henry. Why would he leave his basketball in the basement?"

All that evening and the next morning, Greg imagined what dreadful things could happen between him and Rocco. They were all like a nightmare. His plan was to stay as far away from Rocco as he could. If Rocco were on one side of the playground, he would be on the other side. Amazingly, it worked. In the classroom it seemed like Rocco had forgotten about him. Fortunately, Rocco had to stay after school. The next few days were the same. But Greg was not taking any chances. As far as Rocco was concerned, he stayed as invisible as possible.

Chapter 8

One Saturday morning he went on an errand with his mother. They drove over a bridge and below them was a neat little creek. It was rather wide with sandbars in the middle. Greg loved creeks and decided to come back and explore it later. He considered himself a self-taught expert on creeks. He had explored several creeks near his old home at Riverside, plus an old drainage ditch. The ditch was oil-covered and oozed out from the Ace Chemical Co. He guessed you really couldn't count that one as a creek.

When he arrived home he changed into some grubby clothes and walked back to the bridge. He slid down an embankment to the waters edge. From there he walked upstream as he thought this would take him back toward his house. After a few minutes of walking along the winding bank, he could barely hear the sounds of the traffic. There were lots of big trees and a very narrow path that was somewhat overgrown with weeds. There had been some litter by the bridge: tin cans, bottles, and such. There was none of that now. He reasoned it was too far from human traffic.

As he rounded a bend in the creek, he came upon a very unusual sight. A gigantic tree had fallen across the stream. Half of the roots were still in the ground. Since the tree was getting some nourishment, there were leaves on the branches. Heavy tree limbs were embedded on the opposite side of the creek where the tree landed, keeping the tree trunk out of the water. It was like a bridge and water ran freely under it. Greg wondered how long the tree could live that way.

He decided he would climb onto the tree trunk and walk out over the water. With some effort he hiked himself up and onto the trunk. He then stood up and carefully walked around the branches to where the middle of the creek was about 10 feet directly below. He had never seen a tree in such an unusual position. It gave him an eerie feeling, being in a tree growing out, not up. He was actually walking on the side of a tree!

There was a bend in the creek where the tree had fallen. A raised embankment had been cut away by the current. Greg thought this undercutting of the tree probably caused the tree to fall. He wished that he could have been there to see it. It would have been like seeing a giant lose his balance and slowly come crashing to the earth. At that point the water looked deep, maybe even over his head. On the opposite side and a bit downstream from where the huge branches were embedded in the ground, there was a small beach of sand and gravel. It was a pleasant scene, a quiet place to sit and think. He sat down, leaned against a branch, and watched the water ripple by below him. Everything was quiet and peaceful, unlike the worrisome tensions he faced at school. What a great place for a tree house, he thought.

He decided to scramble back down and gather some rocks and pebbles from the small beach. He would drop them on the few dead leaves bobbing along atop the water below. He would be a bombardier in a B-17 Flying Fortress dropping bombs on German battleships. He went to the beach to gather his ammunition. When his pockets were full he crawled back to his perch in the tree. He waited for a leaf to float by while fingering a pebble. One floated directly under him and he muttered to himself, "Bombs away!" Missed! Quickly, another, and another, and another. The leaf was hurrying downstream now, so he stood up and hurled several more rocks at the target. All misses!

He turned and looked upstream again hoping to spy another "battleship." What got his attention was not some floating leaves he could turn into imaginary battleships, but a turtle! It had hauled himself onto a half-sunken, water-soaked board about a hundred feet away. Greg was quick to name things. The name "Tubby" popped into his head. Yes, Greg thought, he would call it Tubby - Tubby Turtle.

Greg decided to lob a few rocks in that direction to scare it. Then he could watch it swim away. Instead of being a bombardier in a B-17, he would be a soldier firing heavy artillery shells. He threw several rocks. None came close enough to frighten Tubby into moving. This was one brave turtle thought Greg. Maybe he should have called it "Tuffy." His "artillery shells" were all going too far to the left.

He picked out the largest of the rocks so he could get a better grip on it, and thereby throw it more accurately. He made up his mind to keep it right in line with the target, not right, not left, just like he did when he shot baskets. He would hold back on the throw so it would fall a bit short. He relaxed, focused, and hurled the rock.

Perfect! The missile traveled exactly as planned, not right, not left. But as the rock started on its downward path, his satisfaction quickly turned to alarm. He had put too much muscle into the throw. The missile was heading directly for the creature. Under his breath he muttered, "Don't hit it - Please don't!" It did! A *direct* hit. Tubby slipped sideways into the water and disappeared. There were traces of blood visible on the water from where Tubby slid under. Greg felt a pain in the pit of his stomach. How could he, or *anyone*, throw a rock that far and hit such a small object. But it happened. There was nothing he could do to take it back.

He scrambled out of the tree and ran to the spot where the turtle had been. He peered into the water hoping to get a glimpse of the turtle. He could not. He quickly took off his shoes and socks, rolled up his pant legs, and carefully waded into the water. The creek bottom consisted of mud and rock. Each slow step was difficult. After five steps, the water level was to his knees. The water had turned muddy and he could see nothing of the bottom. With each step he could imagine the broken bottle that might be waiting to slice into his foot. It was useless and dangerous. He would go back. He held his arms out to his side to maintain his balance, and began turning around. A series of cautious steps took him back to the shoreline.

Greg did not have a watch, but he knew by the angle of the sun's rays that it was getting late. He reasoned, if he followed the creek further upstream it might take him close to his home. The stream eventually ran to the back of a residential area. It bordered the backyards of some homes he recognized. He cut through a yard and from there it was an easy five minute walk to home. He judged altogether it was about a fifteen minute walk from his home to the tree.

Greg had mixed feelings about his day. As happy as he was to explore the creek and find the tree, he was equally unhappy about hitting Tubby with the rock. Did Tubby live, or was he now lying dead on the creek's bottom, never to sun himself on that board again? Or worse, maybe he was under the water wounded, suffering, and just waiting to die.

At the dinner table he told of exploring the creek and finding the strange tree. He told of climbing out on the tree and how he threw rocks down at the leaves bobbing by on the water below. Greg did *not* tell them of throwing at, and actually hitting, Tubby.

Chapter 9

Miss Johnson called the names of those students whose turn it was to take out the playground equipment. "It's Greg's turn to take out the basketball," she said. Greg got the basketball out of the equipment box. The ball really felt good in his hands and he was eager to take some shots.

Lincoln School had something going for it - 4 baskets on the playground! Not only that, but they had brand new white nets hanging from the rims. Greg had noticed there was usually one or two courts open. He was going to practice shooting all recess, and all by himself. Always wary of Rocco, however, he would keep an eye on him. Rocco had been ignoring him, but Greg had the feeling that would not last.

He took his first shot. Too short. It hit the front of the rim, then the back of the rim, and bounced out. He reminded himself again of what his former coach preached: "If you miss, better to miss long than short. Don't go right, don't go left, don't go short." As he shot the ball, he always pretended it was in a game situation. Of course there was a pretend radio announcer calling the game. "Only seconds to go and Smith has the ball. He shoots, the ball's up - it's, it's, GOOD! Riverside wins again!" Oops, he'd have to change that to Maple City from now on.

Scott, Rocco's friend, called out from another court, "Hey, want to play two on two? Phil and I will stand you and Tom." Scott was a boy with whom he had talked on several occasions. Scott hung around with Rocco a lot, but he seemed okay. Greg had noticed them playing before. Both Scott and Phil were good, but Tom was awkward and inexperienced. "C'mon," Scott urged. "A short game. One point a basket, first team to ten. Here's the ball. You guys can bring it to us. A deal?"

"Yeah, I guess." replied Greg. He really wasn't into a game, but they were here so why not. Greg took the ball out and passed it to Tom. Tom put his nose over the ball, dribbled six times, and threw up an off-balance shot that touched neither rim nor backboard.

"Dang," Tom moaned, "First one I missed all day."

Scott grinned at Greg and joked, "Airball's Tom's specialty. Got pretty classy footwork too, ain't he?"

Phil took the ball out, passed it to Scott, who quickly dribbled around Tom and scored. Tom took the ball out, passed it to Greg who fired a long shot that touched nothing but net. Tom quickly realized that if they were going to have a chance, it would have to be Greg who did all the shooting. Every time he got his hands on the ball he would pass it to Greg. Greg was hitting his shots and it was tied at nine, nine. Phil missed a layup and Tom got the rebound and passed it to Greg. He got ready to put up a long, winning shot, and Scott hollered to Phil, "Don't let him have that shot!" As Phil rushed to guard Greg, Greg faked a shot, then dribbled around him and made a layup for the win.

Scott stood with his hands on his hips and glared at Phil. "My canary plays better defense than that," he said angrily.

Phil said, "Well, Oh Great One, you didn't do any better when you were on him! Looked like you had glue on the bottom of your tennies!"

Tom looked at them, stretched his arms out and said, "No use in arguing about it. Why don't you guys practice up a bit so you get better, and we'll take you on again. Anytime you guys want a rematch just let us know. Just *anytime*! Old Dead-Eye Greg and I will be ready. Won't we Dead-Eye?" Thankfully, the bell rang so it wouldn't be today, thought Greg.

"Ready for another one?" Greg didn't want to answer that one. He shrugged his shoulders and kept walking over to line up. Greg knew the only reason they won was because Scott and Phil were overconfident. Next time would be different. For certain, he did not want a rematch and wished Tom would close his big trap. But he didn't. He kept on yapping about how they beat Scott and Phil.

Greg felt fortunate that every afternoon Rocco had been kept after school. Either he did not have his work done or he had broken some rule. That made an easy trip back home for him, as he didn't have to lookout for Rocco. He wished Miss Johnson would keep him in his cage all year.

At dinner that night, talk was about how the war was going. They talked about the war in the South Pacific. It was there where the U.S. Army, Marines, and the Navy were fighting the Japanese over control of the many small islands in that region. Huge naval battles involving many ships and aircraft took place there. Would Father be sent there? Or would he be sent to Europe to fight the Germans. Maybe he would even be sent to the North Africa desert to fight against the Germans and Italians. Greg could understand why they called it a "World War." It seemed like everybody was fighting everywhere.

The following day when Greg entered the playground, he did his usual search for Rocco. He didn't see him and figured Rocco was late again. Tom came running up from behind him and said, "Hey man, ready to play those guys again? You were just great yesterday. I'd give anything to shoot like that."

"Look Tom," Greg replied, "I can't shoot like that all the time. We got some lucky bounces, and they were overconfident and too sure of a win. They didn't even play hard until the end of the game, and then it was too late. But this time they're going to be ready. I'm not saying we *can't* win but it would be tough. I'm hoping they'll just forget about it."

Tom looked down at his shoes, and without a smile said, "Well, if you put it that way, I guess you're right." But then he said hopefully, "But if we did it once, we *could* do it again."

"Yeah," Greg replied, "But don't be bragging around to everybody how we beat them because that'll just fire them up."

As soon as they stepped into the classroom Scott came over to him and said, "Man did you guys ever clean our clocks yesterday. Today will be different. We'll be ready today! Recess time. Be there!" Tom overheard the message and nodded confidently at Greg and smiled. Greg, however, was *not* ready.

About ten minutes before recess Greg noticed some drops on the windows on the west side. Rain! He hoped it would rain enough to cancel recess. Minutes later the rain poured down in buckets. He was saved, at least for the time being.

The next day brought more rain and more inside recess. Greg had made a few friends so he didn't feel like a complete stranger. Nothing more was said about the basketball game. The thought of playing was fast fading from his mind also, and he was glad about that. All he had to do now was to stay away from Rocco.

At recess inside, checkers was the name of the game. Everybody was either playing or watching. Greg played two games with a girl named Sue and lost both of them. Several classmates were watching. He was an excellent checker player and was surprised when he lost. Nobody else seemed surprised. As he walked away a chubby boy put his hand on his shoulder and said, "Don't feel bad. She beats everybody."

Greg was pleased when she had asked him to play. There were plenty of others she could have asked. Why me, he wondered? She knew everyone, and all the kids seemed to like her. Maybe I'm the only one she hasn't beaten he thought. Or maybe she just wanted me to feel welcomed at Lincoln. Whatever the reason, she *was* an awfully nice girl he thought.

Chapter 10

After school Greg entered the kitchen through the back door of the house. He found his mother reading a letter at the table. He guessed it was from Father and it was. Greg's eyes lit up and he asked, "How's he doing?"

"Well," Mother said, handing the letter to Greg, "why don't you read it yourself. Who only knows, if this war lasts for a long time, you might be in it yourself. You should have at least some idea of what to expect." Greg had never thought about that before.

The part of the letter that stuck in Greg's mind was the following: "We do an hour of exercise before breakfast. This includes running, pushups, situps, squat thrusts, and all sorts of other exercises. I've got to say I'm in the best shape I've ever been in. My muscles are sore, but it's a good soreness, like I'm healthier. I feel great!"

Try as he might, it was hard to imagine Father doing those exercises. He had never seen his father run, except for a few steps when they shot baskets. As for pushups, Greg did fifty in gym class. He wondered how many his father could do.

As he thought of his father, he felt a painful, hollow feeling in his stomach. His eyes felt like they were swelling, as they do before the tears come. But the feeling left quickly, when he remembered what his father had told him about crying. "It's okay to cry," Father had said, "but often it's a matter of only feeling sorry for yourself. Just don't overdue it and let it wear you down."

Then Greg looked at the bright side of the picture: his father was feeling great, and so far he was safe. For that, Greg thought, he should feel thankful. No, Mother was right. We shouldn't be feeling sorry for ourselves. It is Father who is making the real sacrifice.

Bright rays of sunlight shone on the yellow leaves of the maple tree outside his window as he opened his eyes the following morning. Should he roll over and wait for the alarm to ring? No, he thought, it's time to attack the day. He threw back his covers and whirled out of bed, throwing both feet on the floor at the same time. A short time later, with a good breakfast under his belt and his math book in hand, he hustled out the back door. "Don't forget your dental appointment after school," Grandma Henrietta called.

"Yeah, I'll remember," he hollered back, "Wouldn't want to miss all that fun."

Chapter 11

He wasn't three steps onto the playground when someone yelled out, "Here comes our great all-American basketball player. Golly gee! Maybe he'll give me his autograph." It was Rocco. Scott was with him as well as a few others of his followers. They strode over to Greg, and Scott asked, "You ready for that rematch today?" Greg did not reply right away. Scott asked again, "You and Terrible Tom ready for our little get-together? You're not going to chicken out are you?"

"Yeah, we'll play. Why not," Greg answered.

Scott continued, "Phil walked out the door this morning and heaved all over his shoes. He staggered back in the house and fell into his bed. He's just sicker than a dog. Ah, but Rocco here was kind enough to offer to take Phil's place - nice guy that he is."

Greg didn't say anything, but just looked around trying to size up the situation. Scott asked, "Substitutions *are* okay, aren't they?"

Greg said, "You couldn't really call it a rematch if half the team is different."

"Call it whatever you want," Scott said. "If you're afraid to play us we'll just call it off. Oh, *and*, tell everybody you chickened out."

Greg shrugged his shoulders and without a trace of enthusiasm said, "All right, game's on. We'll go with it." The boys in the group all grinned at each other, and Greg knew he had been suckered into a game he could not win.

As the group of boys walked away, Rocco looked back over his shoulder and questioned, "He's too much of a runt to call himself a basketball player, ain't he?" Although the remark was not made to Greg, it *was* intended for Greg to hear.

Greg was close to an average size, but the comment was clearly meant to be a put-down. He ignored it and walked away looking for Tom. He spotted Tom on the other side of the playground being chased by two girls. As Greg arrived, Tom was running in a pattern of figure eights trying to escape from the girls - but not *too* hard. He saw Greg and hollered, "Help! Save me from these monsters." All three of them seemed to tire of the game at the same time and quit to catch their breath.

Tom walked over to Greg and asked, "Hey man, what's going on?"

"You up for the game today?" Greg asked.

"There isn't going to be any game today. Phil's home heaving his guts out," Tom replied.

Greg said, "Scott got Rocco to take his place."

Tom's jaw dropped, and he gave Greg a look of disbelief. Tom exclaimed, "Greg, are you serious? Have you seen Rocco play? He plays basketball like he's in a football game. Man, elbows beating on your ribs all the time. And he's like a Mack truck going for the basket. Get in his way and he just runs you over like you weren't even there. He'll leave his footprints on your *chest*!"

Greg was a little surprised at Tom's response. He seemed determined not to play. "Well," Greg responded, "I've already told them we'd play."

Tom shook his head, looked at Greg, and said, "Man, I figured you to be smarter than that. You should've asked me first. Don't be speaking for me when I'm not there. We can't win and I'm not playing. And that's that!"

Greg was surprised and disappointed at Tom's outburst. But after he considered it, he thought Tom was right. He should *not* have spoken for Tom. "Okay," Greg said, "I'll just go over and tell them you don't want to play and that'll be the end of it." Greg was relieved in a way, to have it over and done with.

He walked over to where Scott and Rocco were standing and found a large group of boys circled around Rocco who was telling a story. He thought he had better not interrupt and waited for Rocco to get through. On and on he went telling about an animal he once trapped.

He finally finished the story, but when he saw Greg he started up all over again. Rocco bragged, "You guys are going to be treated to the game of the century at recess time. My partner Scott and I, are going to take on Terrible Tom and this hotshot new kid here, in a game of two-on-two. The slaughter will take place right over there on that court," and pointed to it with an air of supreme authority. "Be there!" he commanded.

Rocco started to say more but Greg broke in, "Sorry, no game. Tom said he won't play. Sides not fair."

"Now there's one smart guy," Rocco said. "Didn't know ol' Terrible Tom had that many brains. But you go look around. There's got to be some fool around here dumb enough to take you on as a partner. Now get, and go looking, and if you can't find somebody maybe I can come up with an idea."

Greg felt like Rocco had ordered him out. He was thinking he should say something, but instead he just walked away. He felt bad. He wished they'd never come to live here. He wouldn't try and find anybody and hoped that would be the end of it.

Chapter 12

It was a busy morning in class. He wrote so much he dulled his only pencil down to where it made very thick lines. While he was at the pencil sharpener, he heard the old wooden floor creek under the weight of heavy footsteps behind him. Not three inches from his ear, a husky voice quietly said, "Hey, hotshot, have I got a partner for you." Rocco gave Greg a sly smile.

"All right, who is it?" Greg asked.

"Never mind," Rocco said. "Just know it's the tallest one in the class."

Greg gave him a puzzled look and asked, "Who is it, Miss Johnson?"

"Don't worry about it. I'll let you know. Trust me little buddy, I'm going to fix you up really good." Greg had no doubt about that!

A few minutes after Rocco gave Greg the message, Miss Johnson said, "I've got to run to the office for a minute. Behave yourselves and keep working on the assignment I gave you."

As soon as Miss Johnson was out of the room, Rocco stood up, stretched out his arms and said very official like, "May I please have your undivided attention. At recess, all of you will be treated to the basketball game of the century. Your two favorite sports heroes, ahem, myself of course, and my dependable sidekick Scott, will be facing our new, know-it-all hotshot here," pointing to Greg.

"His ever lovin' partner will be the one and only, Leaping Linda Lindstrom." Rocco drew out the name in a sing-songy voice, like a ringmaster in a circus announcing the main act. And that's what the game might turn into thought Greg - a circus. And why had Rocco used the term "ever lovin"? How humiliating!

Greg sat there stunned. Smiles and giggles broke out over the room. Rocco started to say more but Miss Johnson came back. He quickly sat down and the smiles and giggles vanished. Greg felt that everybody was staring at him, and it wasn't his imagination. He wished he could become invisible.

Linda was tall, thin and wiry. She was the fastest kid in the class, boys or girls, but a basketball player she was not. Greg remembered from a gym class just how bad Linda was. In a relay where each player was to dribble to the basket, shoot the ball, and dribble back, the ball hit Linda's feet as often as it did the floor. When she shot the ball, she would bend low, then spring upward and forward. The ball was more likely to go over the backboard than to go through the hoop.

Miss Johnson passed out worksheets she brought back from the office. Greg's mind was not on schoolwork. He was trying to figure a way out of this embarrassing fix. Linda was a sports nut and he knew she would want to play. If he didn't play, *everybody* would feel let down. Before he knew it the worksheets were being picked up. He handed in his blank sheet. Miss Johnson shuffled through the papers, looked up, and asked, "Who handed in the blank paper?" She waved the blank piece of paper over her head for all the class to see. "There's not even a name on it! After all the time I spent giving out the directions on this work, it's hard for me to believe that one of you would turn in a paper without one single mark on it. Nothing. Not a scratch!" She then looked directly at Rocco as if he were obviously the guilty one.

Rocco put his hands on his chest in a defensive manner and said, "It wasn't me. It wasn't me," shaking his head vigorously.

"Rocco, did you hear me accuse *you*?"

Smiling, Rocco said, "No Ma'am, but I know what you're thinking."

Miss Johnson smiled back at him and said, "Well Rocco, it wouldn't be the first time now would it?"

Putting on her more serious face she turned to the class, and again held high the blank sheet of paper. She simply asked, "*Who?*"

Greg raised his hand and said, "Me."

She said, "Greg, that really surprises me. But I guess you've dawdled your way out of recess. Please stay in and complete the paper."

The idea of staying in at recess suddenly became very big in Greg's mind. His problem was solved. Can't play the game if Teacher says I can't go out. He wondered why he hadn't thought of that? It's so simple. Miss Johnson dismissed the class and with a contented smile on his face, Greg began working on the assignment.

As he worked, he had the uneasy feeling he was being watched. He was right. He turned around to see Linda, Scott, and Rocco, arms folded, not just watching, but *glaring* at him.

Miss Johnson was heading out the door for the teacher's lounge, but stopped. She turned around and looked at the three who were eyeing Greg. She asked, "Why are you three so interested in Greg's work?"

As might be expected, Rocco was the first to open his mouth and explain. In his most mannerly voice he begged, "Gee Miss Johnson, you see we planned to have this important basketball game, and it really means a lot to us. Couldn't you let our little friend, Greg here, finish his paper later?"

"Absolutely not," she replied firmly. "Greg thoroughly wasted his time and now he's got to make it up." Several students were poking their heads through the doorway now, wondering if the players in this momentous game were coming out. When she saw them she frowned and said, "Why are you standing there? You're supposed to be on the playground now. Get! Get! Get!"

No sooner had the students in the hall gone, than Mr. Picklehoffer stuck his head in the door. "Miss Johnson," he said, "I hate to take up your recess time, but I've got to talk to you about a private matter." Pointing to the four students still in the room he asked, "Are these students about to leave for recess?"

"All but one," she said.

Seizing an opportunity, Rocco exclaimed, "Oh Miss Johnson, you'd better get rid of ol' Greg here. You wouldn't want him to hear all that private stuff. He can't keep a secret worth a darn. We *all* know that."

Miss Johnson smiled at Rocco. She knew he was kidding around with her, and wanted desperately to extract Greg from the room. "All right, Greg, you've always gotten your work done on time. And since these friends of yours need you so badly for their game, I'm going to give you a big break. You may leave now and do the paper later. Oh, by the way, it's nice to see you and Rocco getting on so well."

Rocco gave Miss Johnson a great big toothy grin and said, "Oh yeah, that Greg here is a great little fellow. Why, we all just love him to pieces."

"One more thing before you go," Miss Johnson added, "I want a full report on the outcome of this big game."

Rocco replied, "Oh I could give you that report right now, but I suppose we should wait until after the game, you know, to make it official."

Greg's hopes to get out of the game had been crushed. But the others were overjoyed and flew into action. Rocco grabbed his arm and, not too gently, lifted Greg from his desk. Linda snatched away his worksheet and pencil and threw them into his desktop. Scott raced out the door and promised to have an empty court waiting for them. Greg felt like a lamb being led to slaughter. All hope was lost.

To make matters even worse, Rocco put his arm around Greg as they walked out of the room. Rocco said, "Man, we were lucky to get you out of there. Bet you'd feel real bad if you couldn't play. C'mon hotshot, why so quiet? Probably saving your breath for the big game eh?"

Although he was late getting out, Scott kept his promise and had an empty court waiting for them. There were several fourth graders walking away from the court. They were looking over their shoulders, scowling, and muttering unkind words about sixth graders. "Told you I'd have a court for us," he bragged. "Just had to sweep off those little munchkins."

There were quite a few onlookers by now. One of them had a ball and tossed it to Rocco. He in turn, threw it to Greg and said, "We've got no time for warm-ups. You guys bring it to us. Oops! I mean girls. Oops again! I mean hotshot and the *Lady.*"

Greg took the ball and passed it to Linda. She bent very low, and with both hands on the ball, sprang forward and let go a shot that sailed high over the backboard. She looked more like a jack-in-the-box than a basketball player. Scott took the ball out and passed it to Rocco. Rocco backed into Linda, forcing her to give ground. When he was nearly under the basket, he turned to his right and made an easy basket.

Greg took the ball out again and passed it to Linda. What happened once - happened again! Linda bent low and shot the ball. It was like a cannon shot and went two feet over the backboard. Again, as in their first play of the game, Scott passed the ball to Rocco. He backed Linda under the basket, pivoted to his right, and made an easy shot.

There were quite a few students watching from the sidelines now. Rocco turned to them, put his hand to his mouth, and faked a yawn. Then he stretched his arms over his head, as one might do when getting out of bed, and said, "Oh hum, I hope I can stay awake for the rest of the game." Many of the onlookers shook their heads and laughed at Rocco's antics.

Greg wondered how he could politely tell Linda to save those shots for another life. To his amazement, as if she had read Greg's mind she said, "I just can't make anything. I'm not taking another shot!"

Scott joked, "Gee Linda, I thought you were doing great. Both shots finally came down and hit the blacktop. I mean, they didn't land up there on the moon."

This time Linda took the ball out. She passed it into Greg and he put up a shot that bounded off the loose rim with a loud clunk. Scott got the long rebound and passed it to Rocco under the basket. Once more, he backed Linda under the basket, turned, and made another easy shot. On the following play Greg put up another shot that bounced off the shaky rim with a sharp clank.

Rocco teased, "Clank clunk, clank clunk, looks like ol' Clank Clunk here can't make the ball fit in the rim." Scott got the rebound and passed it into Rocco who easily scored again.

Greg called Linda aside and said, "Don't let Rocco back you down under the basket next time. Get your forearms up and your elbows out. Stick them right in his back if you have to. Hold your ground."

Linda was tall and thin but she was also strong and quick. Last year at the city track meet she won several events. One of her wins was the long jump, which is how she got the name, "Leaping Linda."

Greg missed another shot. But on the next play when Rocco started backing Linda under the basket, Linda followed Greg's advice and held her ground. She and Rocco had a short shoving match but Linda didn't give an inch. Rocco was surprised and was forced to throw it back out to Scott. He shot the ball and missed. Linda was quicker to the ball than Rocco and got the rebound. She passed it to Greg.

Rocco hollered to Scott, "Don't even guard him. Just stand there and stare at his sissy face." Following Rocco's advice, Scott made no attempt to guard him. Greg took his time and really focused on the shot. Then Scott looked cross-eyed at Greg and stuck out his tongue at him. Greg shot. Clank, another miss!

Rocco turned to the crowd and said, "Maybe we should give him a half point for hitting the rim, you know, like coming close in horseshoes."

Greg never felt more embarrassed in all his life. Rocco was making complete fools of them. Rocco went on bragging, "I think we're going to skunk 'em."

Linda was fuming by now and asked, "What's skunk 'em mean?"

Rocco laughed and said, "It means, Linda - that you make *no* baskets, like in zero, zip, like in doughnut holes. Get the idea? And speaking of skunks, I think your little partner there is shooting like one. He's sure stinking up the court with all those lousy shots he's taking. Ol' Clank Clunk Super Skunk here, couldn't hit an ocean if his toes were in the water." All the kids in the crowd were laughing. The score was 4-0 but no one had left. Rocco was too entertaining!

After a miss by Scott, Greg got the ball and finally scored. Greg felt a surge of confidence when his shot went in. He was a streak shooter and when he got on a roll he was automatic.

"Big deal," Rocco said. "So Skunk made one. That'll be the last one he gets." But it wasn't. With her quickness and jumping ability, Linda was getting most of the rebounds and Greg was starting to hit his shots. They evened the score at 4-4. But despite this, Rocco and

Scott remained overconfident. They continued to laugh and joke around as if they could win the game any time they wanted.

However, before they realized it, the score was tied at eight to eight. It was at this point they became *very* serious. They began arguing over whose fault it was that the game was so close. Rocco said, "Let's switch and I'll take him. I'll put that little skunk in my back pocket."

Scott disagreed and said, "No, you're too slow. He'd be around you before you could blink."

Rocco angrily replied, "Nobody could do worse than you. Look at the score, and Skunk's made *every* basket. *I* will take him and I will *shut him down!*"

Linda took the ball out and passed it to Greg. He faked a shot. Rocco jumped up to block it and Greg easily dribbled around him and scored. After the play, Scott stood there eyeing Rocco up and down. He complained, "Oh great defense partner. Quick feet! You're moving like your shoes are loaded with bricks."

Rocco was so angry he took the ball, raised it high over his head, and with both hands, slammed it on the blacktop. When he let the ball go, he was fully bent over it, and it bounced back and hit him squarely on the nose. Rocco heard the laughter from the kids on the sidelines, and this made him even angrier.

On the next play, Scott passed the ball into Rocco. With a hard shove and a sharp elbow, Rocco was able to get around Linda and score. Some of the crowd on the sidelines cried, "Foul!"

Rocco glared back at them as if to say, "There, take that!"

It was now tied nine to nine and the next basket would win the game. Linda took the ball out and passed it to Greg. Before Greg could get off a shot, *both* Rocco and Scott came over to guard him. They were desperately slapping and clawing for the ball. They had Greg trapped and he could not dribble free. He couldn't see where Linda was, but decided to take a chance. With both hands he hurled the basketball blindly back over his head in the direction of where he thought the basket was. It worked. Linda caught the wildly thrown ball under the basket, and she was free for a shot. Rocco and Scott charged toward her, hollering as loud as they could. The large crowd that had gathered was also yelling excitedly.

Linda put both hands on the ball and went into her usual jack-in-the-box crouch. Greg was certain she would propel the ball into Canada. But this time she used the backboard. The ball hit high on the backboard. The basketball came down and bounced from one side of the rim to the other - and off! By now both Rocco and Scott were there. All three of them went high for the rebound, but Leaping Linda came down with the ball. Immediately, she got off another shot, despite the fact that Rocco whacked her on her arm as she shot the ball. The ball bounced from one side of the rim to the other as it did before. But then it rolled slowly around the edge of the rim and almost stopped. It was as if the ball had a mind of its own and was trying to decide which way to fall. And then it did. It fell IN!

The crowd reacted wildly. Some clapped. Some shook their heads in disbelief. The *girls* were *very* happy at the outcome. One girl shouted, "And Leaping Linda scores the winning basket!" They crowded around Linda, congratulating her on the shot.

A few told Greg, "Great game," but the bell had rung and every-one was hurrying to line up. Greg was happy to see Linda getting most of the attention. He just wanted to disappear. He knew Rocco would rather swallow a can of worms than lose a game like this. The embarrassing loss would give him yet more reason to get even.

Miss Broadaxe was on recess duty. Students were always mak-ing jokes about Miss Broadaxe, who was very strict. The jokes usu-ally had something to do with "chopping," something like, "Old Miss Broadaxe will make you a foot shorter at the top if you don't behave." Her name "Broadaxe" fit her well. She had that broad, linebacker-look, and a sharp tongue. She shielded her eyes from the sun and peered out onto the playground. She frowned and asked, "Who is sitting out there in the middle of the basketball court?" Everyone turned to look. Several students answered at the same time. Through the high-pitched jabber that followed, the teacher understood it was Rocco. He was sitting cross-legged on the court, with his elbows on his knees. He was staring at the blacktop with a blank look on his face. It was a strange sight, the single figure, sitting there staring at nothing.

With a voice stronger than a hog caller at a county fair, Miss Broadaxe exploded, "Rocco Hardknuckle, you get your sorry looking fanny off that blacktop and line up!" When Rocco didn't move a muscle to get up, she charged out after him like a raving rhino. Seeing Miss Broadaxe, pounding over the blacktop towards him, Rocco got moving. He gave her a whining, "I'm coming, I'm coming." Huffing and puffing, her face red with anger, she returned to the front of the lines and dismissed the students to their classes.

As Greg entered the classroom the kids were still talking about the game. Miss Johnson picked up on this and said, "My, that must have been one whale of a game. Who won?"

One of the girls exclaimed, "Linda won!" And the girls went on to tell Miss Johnson about the game.

"But where's Rocco?" Miss Johnson asked.

The same girl who gave Linda credit for winning the game laughed and said, "Oh, he's sitting out there in the middle of the playground pouting because he lost the game."

At this point Miss Broadaxe came to the door. She said, "Miss Johnson, a student of yours, that being a Mr. Hardknuckle, believes he's entitled to a bit more recess time than everyone else in this school. Here's *everybody* lined up to go in, and *he's* sitting out there in the middle of the basketball court still soaking up the sunshine."

Rocco was lurking beyond the doorway, out of sight. But everyone could hear him strongly protest, "I came in, now didn't I ?"

"Yes you did, but only after my special invitation. What if I had to go around to a hundred or more kids, who were also sitting on the playground enjoying the sunshine, and give each one a special invitation to come in?" Miss Broadaxe continued in a mocking tone of voice, "Oh, Miss so-and-so, would like to line up now. Please? It's time to go in. And say the same thing to another, and another, and another. I'd rather herd cattle!" Turning back to Miss Johnson she said, "Mr. Hardknuckle will be my guest after school today, Miss Johnson." Greg was thankful. He would have a safe passage after school today. That was good because he had enough painful things to worry about with his dentist appointment coming up.

Chapter 13

At the dinner table, all the talk was of Mother's interview at the Happy Toy Co. Mother said, "I've never had a real job interview before." Looking at her parents she said, "Remember the job I had at Ann's Cafe? They just knew me and asked me if I wanted to wait tables for them. And later, when I was a senior in high school, I worked at Floyd's grocery store. And you got me that job. You told me your old friend Floyd was looking for someone to work at his store. I just walked over there and he put me to work that afternoon. There were no forms to fill out or anything like that."

Greg asked, "So what did you have to do today?"

"Well I had to fill out two pages of questions," Mother answered. "Then the personnel manager, Mr. Turner, looked at the completed papers and asked me a few more questions. He said the work would be hard, and the place would be noisy. He said a lot of women quit after the first few days. He encouraged me to stick with it, and it would get easier as I got used to it. Oh, he also told me to give you a big hello, Dad."

"Yeah, old Joe Turner and I worked on the production line for several years," Grandpa Henry said. "Then he started getting promotions and finally ended up head man in the Personnel Department. When I called him and told him you were coming over to apply for a job, we had a nice long talk about the old days. Yeah, ol' Joe's a good guy."

Mother said, "Mr. Turner said I'd be getting a letter from the company about the job. He kind of talked like I already had the job, but didn't actually say that."

Grandpa Henry laughed and said, "Oh, don't worry Rose, you'll get the job."

Mother replied, "Well I don't know about that. There were about a dozen people waiting for interviews when I left."

Grandpa Henry dismissed the idea with a wave of his hand and said, "He'll probably hire all of them."

Grandma Henrietta said, "Well, honey, Mr. Turner is right when he encouraged you to stick with it for awhile, but don't kill yourself. There's other work to be found. Your health is more important than money. We'll get by okay regardless of whether you get the job or not."

"It's good money," Mother replied, "and it's a challenge. We'll just wait and see how it goes. Besides, the more I can do to support the war effort, the more I'm supporting Will. And I want my husband back!"

Chapter 14

As Greg walked to school the next day, he tried to think of all the bad things that could happen between Rocco and him. He wanted to be prepared for the worst. After yesterday, Rocco would have *more* reason to want to squeeze him till his eyeballs pop out and roll on the ground with the ants.

Just when he reached the playground, he was startled by the noise of a bike racing up from behind him. He braced himself for the worst, the "worst" of course being Rocco. Instead, it was Scott. He braked the bike hard, skidding the back tire on the blacktop. Greg thought Scott might be angry judging the way he brought the bike to a screeching halt. But he wasn't. He just said, "Hey Greg, wadda you know?" Scott was riding a rather new looking black and gold, Schwinn "Liberty" bike. It was a top of the line bike, and very expensive. Back home in Riverside there was one just like it displayed in a store window for thirty-six dollars. How he had wanted that bike!

Scott's bike looked almost new. Greg said, "What a great bike!"

"Thanks," Scott replied. "Dad bought it for me right before the Schwinn Bicycle Co. stopped making them. This might be the last one they made. Dad said I'd better take good care of it because they sure won't be making anymore till after the war. They're making war stuff now."

"You got a bike?" Scott asked.

"No, not right now at least. I had one, but we didn't have room for it when we moved. Besides, the brakes were shot. I tried to fix them. Had bike parts all over the garage floor. Dad helped me put it back together, but they still didn't work right."

"Well, I gotta be parking my bike," and he rolled it over to the bike rack. Greg was surprised that Scott stopped to talk with him. Greg figured Scott would be angry about their loss yesterday. After Scott parked his bike, he hurried to catch up with Greg. He brought a yo-yo out of his pocket to show Greg. Yo-yos were being sold in many of the stores around the town and kids were buying them.

Scott said, "I just bought this thing a couple days ago and I can already do a double loop." Several other boys came over to watch. Another boy joined them and brought out a yo-yo, as did another boy. Soon there was a circle of kids doing their yo-yo tricks and talking about the merits of different kinds of yo-yos.

Out of the corner of his eye Greg could see Rocco approaching the group. When the other boys saw Rocco swaggering toward them with his long stride, they stepped back to let him in the circle. It was as if some four star general had arrived, and everybody stopped and waited for their orders.

"Hey guys," he announced, "guess what? I got a dog! Yeah, it's a little beagle pup. He's got big ol' floppy ears so I named him "Floppy." My ma doesn't like him. He's not housebroken yet so when I'm not there she's got to clean up the mess. She said she'll give him one more week. After that he's going to be wearing diapers. Myself, I can't picture a dog in diapers. Can you? But that's what she said. She gets mad as heck when he gets in her way. She'll pick him up by the ears and throw him out of the kitchen. Says it doesn't hurt him. Bet she'd howl if somebody picked *her* up by the ears and threw *her* out of the kitchen!"

Then Rocco stood with his hands on his hips eyeing the yo-yos.

With all the bluster he could muster Rocco announced, "I guess we all know who's king of this yo-yo stuff don't we?" Without waiting for an answer he went on, "C'mon who's going to loan me a yo-yo so you can see how an expert does it?" Again, neither waiting nor expecting an answer, Rocco grabbed a yo-yo out of someone's hand. He turned it over in his hands and inspected it. He shook his head and thrust it back into the boy's hand. Rocco snapped at him, "This is gotta be the *cheapest*, the *ugliest,* yo-yo on the planet. My dog wouldn't want that thing to chew on. Looks like something your grandpa whittled out of a rotten corncob with a dull pocket knife."

"C'mon, somebody give me a good one so I can show you my magic." One of the smaller boys in the group offered his yo-yo to Rocco and said proudly, "Just bought this doozy for two and a half bucks. It's all metal not wood."

Rocco grabbed it and looked it over carefully. "Yep, pretty good. Pretty *darn* good." He inspected it once more, eyed the boy and said, "Looks just like the one I lost the other day. Say, you haven't been sneaking around my house lately, have you?"

The small boy assumed Rocco was kidding, but still didn't know exactly how to respond to the question. He also wondered whether he'd get his yo-yo back. He needn't have worried about a response, because before one word could ever get out of his mouth, Rocco was into his yo-yo routine. It was an impressive array of yo-yo stunts and ended with a double loop.

"There," Rocco said, "Who can top *that*?" He called out the names of some of the boys in the group and offered them the yo-yo as a challenge. Not one stepped forward to accept. Rocco's performance was one not many could match anyway. More importantly, whoever in their right mind would want to do better than Rocco and show him up?

Chapter 15

Then Rocco's eyes turned on Greg. Greg had stood back a bit, so as not to be noticed. It didn't work. "Ah ha! I see my little nuisance friend is trying to hide. But I, like the Shadow, sees all, knows all." The Shadow, to whom Rocco referred, was a popular radio program of the day. The Shadow could make himself invisible and then solve crimes. He was noted for a very evil, long, drawn out laugh. After the scary laugh came the words, "What evil lurks in the hearts of men? The Shadow knows." Then he would do that mysterious sounding laugh again.

Rocco went into a very good imitation of what a character like the Shadow might do. He bent over in a crouch, chin forward, and all ten fingers stretched out in a pointing position. He walked slowly around the inside circle of boys. With his eyes opened wide he stared at each one as he passed by. "Yeah," Rocco continued, "Sees all, knows all. Ah ha! The Shadow knows," he repeated in a low threatening voice. He followed the words with a very good copy of the Shadow's long wicked laugh.

And then those piercing eyes stopped and focused directly on Greg. Rocco straightened up and switched out of his pretend Shadow character, and in a very normal voice said, "I think it's your turn now." Rocco thrust the yo-yo into Greg's hand.

Not wanting to provoke Rocco, Greg quietly said, "Naw, looks like your the yo-yo champ."

Greg held the yo-yo out to return it to him. Rocco ignored the yo-yo and turned to the gathering crowd. He pleaded his case to the group, stretched out his arms, palms up, and said, "Now I ask you, here's a new kid in our school and Teach says we should be nice to him. Right? So I ask him to join in our fun and he refuses! That's like he's being a stuck-up little snob. Right?"

It was clear to Greg that Rocco was trying to get the crowd riled up against him. For the most part, however, the onlookers seemed not swayed by Rocco's talk, although a few made some nasty remarks. Greg decided to remain silent, and see what Rocco would do next. Turning back to Greg, Rocco put his hands on his hips, and leaned forward into Greg's face. In a commanding voice he said, "Try it!"

Greg was determined not to lose his cool. Never mind that he could make a yo-yo do everything but talk. What Greg could do with a yo-yo would make Rocco look like a beginner. But he was still not angry enough to show Rocco up. By now it felt like a fight scene, as he was completely encircled by the crowd. All he wanted to do is get out of this mess.

He carefully put the end loop of the yo-yo string on his index finger and let the yo-yo drop and brought it back up. "Well, that's about it," he said. He took the string off his finger and handed it back to Rocco.

"That's all?" questioned Rocco in pretended amazement. Rocco smiled and looked at the group and said, "C'mon, a two year old with filled diapers could do better than that." The remark brought a laugh from the spectators. Rocco got back into Greg's face and said, "Me and the guys here want to see you do it *three* times. Don't we guys?"

One boy in the crowd hollered, "Yeah, then maybe we can promote him to a three year old." There were some other taunts from the crowd now, and Greg knew Rocco had succeeded in turning most of the boys against him.

Rocco said, "Not so fast. We want you to do it with this old wooden contraption." Rocco then threw the string of the old yo-yo around Greg's head and handed it to him. Greg put the other yo-yo in his pocket and slowly untangled the string from around his head with his free hand.

He'd had enough: enough from that smart-mouthed bully Rocco, enough from the taunting crowd. He coolly looked over the mob of kids. He then looked Rocco straight in the eye and asked, "Three times huh?"

Greg calmly said, "Well, let's see if I can get this ol' beast of a yo-yo cranked up to do something." He put his finger in the loop of the string and let the yo-yo fall once. He smiled and looked at Rocco, as he let it slowly fall a second time. Then he turned to the onlookers and, still smiling, let it fall a third time. He was going to enjoy this *very* much.

Then he said to no one in particular, "Let's see if I can get this old piece of rotten wood airborne." This he did, in a very graceful loop. Then he did a double loop. While keeping the old yo-yo going, he brought the other one out of his pocket and somehow got that one going also. The crowd was stunned into absolute silence. He did several tricks, that were difficult enough with only one yo-yo, let alone two. He ended his performance with an impressive 2 yo-yo super double loop.

He stopped. He handed them back to their owners. He turned to Rocco and simply said, "You're right about the old wooden one. It's got a mind of its own. It's slow and hard to control." Everyone was quiet, still in a state of shock. The bell rang and the crowd

moved toward the building to line up. Greg could now hear mur-
murings among them.

One in the group said, "Wow! What a show!" Another said,
"That's unbelievable!" Some were shaking their heads in astonishment. The crowd hummed of Greg's incredible skill. Rocco was
scowling and said nothing.

Scott caught up with Rocco and said, "Man, did you see that?"

"Yeah, yeah, yeah. I saw that all right." Rocco didn't want to
give up an inch of ground in his dislike of Greg, and for sure didn't
want to give him *credit* for anything. Rocco continued, "Everybody's got to be good at *something*. I got a score to settle with that
little jerk and believe me I'm going to come out a winner on this
one."

Scott shook his head and said, "Man, I don't know about that.
Rocco, face it, he just made a fool out of you back there. It's like
he's always one step ahead of you - every time."

Rocco frowned at Scott and shot back, "Just shut up on it will
you?"

Chapter 16

It was an easy walk home, as he did not have to watch out for Rocco. Rocco was busy again after school, doing the work he failed to get done during the regular school hours. Greg thought that was very convenient. It would please him greatly if Rocco would goof off every day and never get his work done.

Upon returning home, Grandma Henrietta put Greg right to work. She said, "Go up and change your clothes. Put on some old pants because I want you to go out and help your grandfather weed the garden. And if you don't come back from the garden dirty, I'll know you didn't work hard enough."

Grandpa Henry saw Greg coming and got up. He said, "This is our "Victory Garden."

"Looks pretty good," Greg replied.

"Yep," Grandpa Henry said, "but it sure does take a lot of work. Come over here and I'll show you what I'm doing." Greg stooped over, hands on knees and watched. "Now this is a carrot top and everything else is a weed," Grandpa Henry explained, showing Greg the lacy looking carrot top.

Greg began to pick the weeds. "No, no no," Grandpa Henry said. "You can't do the job by just bending over like that. After five minutes it'll feel like you're carrying a piano on your back. No, you've got to get those knees down in the dirt." Greg did as he was told, and Grandpa Henry said, "That's it. Getting in the dirt is good for you. It'll make you feel like you're a part of the garden."

As they worked together pulling out the pesky weeds, Grandpa Henry said, "Say Son, your mother said you didn't have room to bring your bike here. You want another one?"

Greg's eyes brightened up at the thought of another bike and said, "Sure do! But Mom said it would be awhile because we don't have the money right now."

"Well now, have I got a deal for you. There's a Mrs. Sutter who lives across the street and down a few houses. Her son's gone and won't be needing it anymore. She knows you moved in with us. Grandma and her are real good friends and they talk a lot. Well, she said you could have the bike. But I told her you'd do a few chores for her now and then whenever something comes up. That seems more fair to me."

"Sounds good to me too," replied Greg.

Grandpa Henry continued, "She just lives across the street and down a couple of houses. It's a small gray bungalow, the only house on that side of the street with a star in the window. You know, the star means somebody in the home is in the service." Greg knew, because several homes in his old neighborhood displayed them.

After his work in the garden, he went looking for Mrs. Sutter's house. He found it and knocked on the front door. A tired look-ing middle aged woman appeared. She was dressed in slacks that were a bit soiled, and wore a bandana over her hair. She looked like someone who had just come in from gardening. She smiled graciously and said, "I'll bet you're Greg, Henry and Henrietta's grandson coming to look at the bicycle."

"Well yes I am," Greg replied.

"Come in Greg, and I'll show you the old bike. It's down in the basement. Please excuse the way I look. I just got home from work and haven't had a chance to freshen up yet. Henrietta said your mom applied for a job at the same place I work, the Happy Toy Co."

"Yes, but she hasn't heard anything from them yet." he replied.

"Oh she will," Mrs. Sutter replied. "The company is expanding and needs more workers."

Greg followed Mrs. Sutter to the basement. He was stunned to see it was the same Schwinn Liberty bike that Scott had, only a bit older. And it was the same as the one he envied in the store window in Riverside. All three bikes were black with gold trim and would be difficult to tell them apart if set side by side. The bike was well-cared for and altogether much more than he had expected.

Mrs. Sutter said, "I've dusted it off and put air in the tires with this old bike pump. Looks like everything works fine on it. Let's get it up and out of here so you can try it."

They bounced it up the basement stairs and outdoors. Greg mounted the bike and circled around the street with it. The seat was a bit high but other than that it was perfect.

He rode back to where Mrs. Sutter was standing and said, "This is really, really nice of you to give me this bike. And Grandpa Henry said you might have some chores for me to do now and then."

"As far as I'm concerned I intended to just give it to you," Mrs. Sutter replied. "But your Grandpa Henry had a different take on it. He said kids should learn that nothing is free. Kids should earn what they get. So he volunteered you to do some things for me once and a while."

"Yep," Greg replied as he gazed admiringly at this new prize. "Just let me know. Got anything you need done now?"

"Well, yes I do." she replied. "There's a couple of little jobs you could help me with."

With some effort he shook off his gaze from his new found treasure and turned to look at Mrs. Sutter.

They went back in the house and he helped Mrs. Sutter move two pieces of furniture and then hung a picture for her.

When done with these tasks, Greg noticed a large picture of a young man in a leather flight jacket standing by a B-17 Flying Fortress. Just below the cockpit was painted, "Molly's Angel."

Greg asked, "Is that your son?"

"Yes," answered Mrs. Sutter. "That picture was taken somewhere in England. He's the pilot."

"Oh wow!" Greg exclaimed. "I know all about that plane. I wrote a report on it last year for class. What I wouldn't give to be a tail gunner on a plane like that. I even built a model of the plane and showed it to the class when I gave the report."

Mrs. Sutter said, "I'm the 'Molly' the plane is named for. He's not allowed to say much in his letters. You know the slogan, 'The enemy might be listening.' He's been over there a long time now and he's flown a lot of missions. So far he's always come back. I think about him everyday. As we stand here speaking, he could be flying over Germany. Yes, right at this very moment." A look of concern showed in her face and she closed her eyes for just a few seconds. But then she recovered and with a smile said, "I'm sorry Greg, I shouldn't be spilling out all my worries on you." And still smiling she said, "Well, you know how mothers worry. Right?"

"Oh no, I'm glad you told me about him," Greg said. Greg was impressed and said, "I can't *believe* that I'll be riding his old bike! Tell him I'll take good care of it."

Then Greg remembered the writing project Miss Johnson assigned the class. Greg said, "We have a writing assignment in our English class. We're supposed to write to someone who's in the service, but someone who's not a relative. You know, like a neighbor or somebody like that. You think I could write to your son?"

Mrs. Sutter's face brightened, "Oh my goodness, yes! You sure could. He's always ready for mail. I'll get the address and write it out for you. Just a moment." She left the room and returned with the address.

"Well Greg," she said, "I'm so tired I'm going to have to lie down and rest before I make dinner. That factory work is hard! I do hope you will enjoy the bike."

Greg bid her goodbye and thanked her one more time for the bicycle. He quickly hopped on his new bike and took it for a test run. It was a quiet street and he felt safe to make some wide turns: a wide turn left, a wide turn right, left again, right again. There was a comfortable rhythm in the repeated motion.

Pretending he was flying a B-17, he made a wide turn left and made a rat-a-tat-tat machine gun noise. He imagined continuous bursts of antiaircraft shells exploding around him. "Bombs away!" he said to himself. "Time to make my turn and fly back to the base." All guns were blazing back at the Nazi fighter planes swarming around him - rat-a-tat-tat, rat-a-tat-tat.

He pulled the curtain on that imaginary scene and thought again of his new bike and the B-17 pilot to whom it once belonged - *that* pilot riding on *this* bike. Unbelievable!

He told his mother about his writing assignment and his plan to write to Capt. Sutter.

Mother said, "That certainly is a worthwhile assignment. Miss Johnson seems like a very creative teacher."

Greg asked, "Do you have any stationary I can use?"

Mother answered, "Why don't you use V-Mail."

"What the heck is that?" Greg replied.

Mother said, "I'll show you." She went to another room in the house and returned with some small preprinted sheets of paper.

She said, "The U.S. Postal Service wants people to write on these. When you're done they can be folded and made into their own envelopes. Clever huh?"

"Why?" Greg questioned.

"Saves space," Mother answered.

"So?" Greg asked.

"So the government has more room to ship war materials."

Grandpa Henry, who happened to be walking through the room, stopped and said, "I just read an article in a magazine about that V-Mail stuff. They'll take a picture of your letter and shrink it some way. It's on something called microfilm. Then, after it gets across the ocean to where it's going, they enlarge it so you can read it. Goes airmail. Lots faster than a ship. Almost two thousand letters can be put in a package that you can hold in the palm of your hand. Amazing!"

Mother said, "See all that extra space leaves more room for war materials."

Greg said, "Got it."

He took the stationary offered by Mother and went to his room to write the letter.

He sat down at his table with the V-Mail stationary and began to write. Greg was puzzled as to how to address him. If he began, "Dear Steve," it would suggest they already knew each other, which they didn't. He decided to address it to "Capt. Steve Sutter."

Greg wrote about how he met his mother, Molly, and getting the bike. He thanked him for the bike and promised to take good care of it. He asked about the plane and what it was like to fly a bomber in combat with everybody shooting at him. He asked him other questions and was surprised to see how much he had written in such a short time.

At dinnertime, Greg was quick to tell everyone how much he liked his new bike. He told them about the letter he wrote to Capt. Sutter and seeing the picture of him standing in front of his B-17 bomber, "Molly's Angel."

Grandma Henrietta said, "He was always such a nice boy. I just hope his luck holds out and he returns home safely."

Grandpa Henry said, "And talk about a basketball player, when Steve was a senior in high school, Maple City won the conference. Boy, could he shoot the ball. Maybe when he gets home he can give you a few tips. He was a good football player also. Yes sirree, you throw that ball up in the air and Steve would come down with it. When the starting quarterback went down with a knee injury they gave Steve the job. That was in the middle of the season and Maple City didn't lose a game after that. He was smart. Made good decisions. That's what good quarterbacks have to do. And he could do it! Just like he's quarterbacking the crew of that B-17 now."

Mother turned to Greg and asked, "You've not said anything about school lately. How do you think you're doing?"

Greg replied, "Pretty good I think. I turned in a book report today and I think it's a winner."

Startled, Grandma Henrietta said, "Dinner! You just *ate* it!"

Grandpa Henry smiled, looked at his wife and said with a chuckle, "Henrietta, Greg didn't say anything about *dinner*. He said he thinks he's getting *thinner*." Grandpa Henry laughed, "Must be all that work he did in the garden."

Grandma Henrietta shook her head disapprovingly and scolded, "Henry, Greg put a lot of work into that garden today so I don't think it's right to call him a *beginner*!"

Grandpa Henry ignored her response and said, "Why don't you make some of those corn fritters like you used to. That'd fatten him up. Boy were they good!"

Mother smiled and said, "Excuse me. I think I'll drink my coffee on the porch."

Greg didn't know where to begin to straighten things out and said, "I think I'll shoot some baskets."

Grandma's eyes lit up and she said, "Oh, you've found your basketball! Good for you. I'll bet you didn't find it in the basement."

Chapter 17

On a pleasant day after school he decided to revisit the creek. Upon arriving, the first thing he did was to look for Tubby. He wondered again, whatever happened to the turtle. Tubby was nowhere to be found.

Now the creek was covered with many different colored leaves: red, brown, orange, yellow, and all shades in between. No rain had fallen for days so the water was low and still. The leaves moved slowly downstream like colorful, tiny boats. Greg looked down at the scene from his perch in the tree. He pretended that they were ships and they all were heading out of the harbor and into battle. He had taken some small pebbles out on the branch with him. Carefully selecting one of the biggest "ships" as a target, he let go of one of his pebble, "bombs." A miss! Another shot, another miss. He had to stop that ship! It was the flagship of the fleet. He let go three at a time, all misses. With a fistful of pebbles, he let go of them all at once. The volley of rock sprayed the surface of the creek like a machine gun. All misses. At that, he decided to climb back to shore and get some heavy artillery. He spied a half a brick and two good sized rocks. As he began climbing back toward the bank to get the heavier ammunition, a very familiar girl's voice drifted to his ears.

"Greg, what in the world are you doing over here?" It was Sue, the checker champ.

Greg thought it was embarrassing to be caught in the act of playing make-believe war games. He decided he'd better not admit it.

"Oh, nothing. Just throwing a few rocks in the creek," he replied nervously.

It seemed strange to see Sue outside of the school setting. Of course, it always seemed strange to see *anyone* outside of the places you normally see them.

Sue said, "I've never seen you around here before. Do you live close by?"

"Yeah, pretty close," he replied. Greg really didn't know what to do, or say. He always felt uncomfortable talking with girls, and especially with Sue. Now, thought Greg, here I am stuck out in the woods with her.

"Which way do you live?" she asked.

Greg pointed and said, "Over that way a few blocks. It's on Eastern Avenue."

"How did you *ever* find this place?" she asked. "Nobody ever comes here."

"I spotted the creek from a bridge a few blocks away and decided to come back later to explore it. If nobody ever comes here, how did *you* ever find it?" he asked.

"Because I live right over there," she replied, and pointed to the direction of her house.

"Hey, you live in a real neat spot with the creek so close," he replied.

Sue wanted to know more about Greg's experience in exploring creeks. He told her about his adventures in Riverside where he followed every stream in the area to where they emptied into the Muskrat River. He even told her about the one where he had to follow it through a long, round tunnel which ran under a highway. You could only do it when the water was low, and then you had to jump from rock to rock and from side to side to avoid getting soggy shoes.

She also asked him what life was like in his old home town of Riverside, and the reasons for his move to Maple City. After a good length of time, Sue excused herself. "I've got to run now," she said.

"Where are you going," Greg asked, "home to practice your checkers?"

Sue laughed, "C'mon, Greg, I don't practice checkers. I just make a few lucky moves now and then, that's all."

Greg watched her climb down from the tree and struggle up the steep bank. Then he thought about their conversation. She was really easy to talk with, he thought. But when he stopped to think about it again, he realized that it was *he* who was doing all the talking. All Sue did was ask questions and listen. Anyway, he felt good about their chance meeting.

For a week or more, Rocco had not been a problem. Rocco had ignored Greg and he, Greg, had stayed clear of Rocco.

October was warm and the leaves were turning into their brilliant colors. Maple City was well-named, thought Greg. The maple trees gave the city rich fall colors. He looked out of the opened schoolroom window as he sharpened the pencil. Oh how he wished he could free himself from these four walls. But his math paper waited for him. He had to get his brain and his pencil together and crank out correct answers. Twenty-five three digit multiplication problems were assigned. They were to do as many as they could in 20 minutes. As he sat down to work, the smell of the beautiful October morning kept pulling his mind away from his math. The air was like a magnet. Only when he gathered up every ounce of his mental muscle could he begin making some marks on the empty paper. He did it. The first two problems were agony. After that, his mind got into it and it became easier.

As he was walking home after school, he found himself adding up all the events since moving to Maple City. He liked Miss Johnson and the class all right. Still, he would trade it all in a moment to go home. He wondered how long he would have to live here before he would call it home. He was not unhappy. Generally, life in his new home was good. There was only one real problem, the loud, overgrown bully, Rocco "The Rock" Hardknuckle.

That problem was still not solved, and he and Linda had made it worse by beating Rocco and Scott. There was no talk of a rematch by either of them. Partly he thought, because Rocco and Scott could never take the chance of being humiliated again. The yoyo embarrassment didn't help either.

Also, everybody was into kickball now. No one had forgotten the "Linda" game, however. Although several days had passed, Rocco had not spoken once to Greg. He never did speak much to him anyway, but now he was going out of his way not to speak to him. Only once did Greg hear him mention his name. It was when he, Greg, got the highest score in class on a quiz. Miss Johnson announced that fact to the class. On the way out to recess, Rocco said to Scott, loud enough for Greg to hear, "Skunk's head will be so big he won't be able to get out the door."

It was a put-down Greg thought, but not life threatening. Little did Greg know, the very next day would see the two of them on a collision course once more.

Chapter 18

The following day, the bell signaling the recess period was not as jarring as usual. Sometimes it rang unexpectedly and would come as a jolt to some of the more hard working students who were lost in their work. But it was no surprise today. *Everybody* was watching the clock and mentally counting down the last seconds till the bell. The name of the game at recess was now kickball. Most of the kids were playing and they were having some of the best kickball games of their lives. All the games had been close with lots of action.

"The kickball goes to Rocco today," Miss Johnson announced. "The jump rope goes to Judy, the softball to Ted and the football to Scott."

"We don't need anything but the kickball," Rocco explained.

He was right. When the class was dismissed, all that was gone was the kickball. The rest of the equipment lay rejected in the equipment box.

The sides were already made up so they could run out and stake a claim to a diamond and begin playing.

After several minutes of play, the team Greg was on had scored several runs. Rocco was on the opposing team and hadn't even been up yet. Rocco's team was doing poorly in the field and even Rocco had made an error. He was everywhere though, trying to get the third out so his team could be up. They would have to hurry because recess only lasted 20 minutes.

"Oh, no!" cried Rocco, "Not ol' Super Skunk again. Kick it with both feet this time. Maybe it will go twice as far."

The pitcher was anxious to get the last out and was angry the other team had scored so many runs. Her anger showed in the next pitch. It was fast and bouncy. Greg kicked it anyway, but the ball went off the outside of his foot, high into the air and drifted over, and onto the roof of the old school. Worse, it did not come down. It got stuck among some leaves which were piled up against the drain spout.

Rocco exploded. He threw the full force of his anger at Greg, "Nice going, you meathead, now we won't get to finish the game because of you. Thanks heaps, for nothing! Who's the teacher on duty?" he asked to anyone who would answer.

"Miss Broadaxe, but I don't see her," someone replied.

Another player laughed and remarked, "She probably got busy beating up on her kids and forgot about her recess duty."

Eyeing the roof with a look of determination, Rocco said, "I'm going up."

Scott warned Rocco, "You'd better not get caught on that roof. They threw Joe Applebee out of school for three days for going up there."

"I know what I'm doing," he shouted as he ran for the door. "You just hold that diamond for us until I get back with the ball."

In the meantime, Greg, feeling responsible for the kickball being on the roof, found a softball and began throwing it at the stuck kickball. The school building was an old 2 1/2 story brick structure which made the gently pitched roof extremely high off the ground. It was all Greg could do to throw the ball that high, let alone aim it. After a couple of minutes and several throws, he decided to give it one last heave. He let it go with all his might. The softball sailed to the roof of the building and, miracle of miracles, it hit the kickball. As the ball began a slow roll to the edge of the roof, two unfortunate events happened. First, Rocco appeared on top of the roof. Secondly, the principal, Mr. Picklehoffer, came out the door and asked some children if they had seen Miss Broadaxe. They said they had not seen her since she gave little Larry Larson six swats on the west stairway for thumbing his nose at her.

As Mr. Picklehoffer walked along the side of the building looking for Miss Broadaxe, the ball came falling from the roof. He stopped right under the falling ball and turned to look for his missing playground teacher. The ball *and* Mr. Picklehoffer's head had a perfect meeting. It hit him squarely in the center of his head. So direct was the hit that it bounced not left, not right, but straight back up in the air. Then it came back down and hit him directly on the noggin a *second* time.

The force of the falling ball drove Mr. Picklehoffer's hat down over his ears. His glasses were knocked to the very end of his nose. At that moment, high atop the school, Rocco walked to the edge of the roof. He hadn't seen Greg throw the softball that jarred loose the kickball. Nor, had he seen Mr. Picklehoffer get beaned twice by the ball. Rocco looked out over the playground and really felt good about making his climb to the roof. It was as if he had just scaled a mountain peak. He was not only on top of the school, he felt as though he was on top of the world. He felt so wonderful he decided to celebrate. He took a deep breath, and while beating on his chest, let out a thunderous Tarzan yell, "Ow-ee-ow, ow-ee-ow."

All the kids on the playground heard the hoot, stopped their playing instantly, and stood there as if frozen, gaping at Rocco. Mr. Picklehoffer struggled with both hands to lift his hat back off his ears, then slid his glasses back up to his eyeballs. Hearing the yell, he looked skyward in time to see Rocco thumping on his chest and bellowing out a second Tarzan roar. Midway through his yell, however, Rocco saw the very angry Mr. Picklehoffer glaring at him. As their eyes met, Rocco's mighty holler faded into a helpless groan.

The ape-like chest thumping stopped right in the middle of a good thump. Suddenly, Rocco did not seem to know where to put his arms. He looked at his fists, unclenched his fingers and rather awkwardly put his hands behind his back. They stared at each other for a full 17 seconds before Mr. Picklehoffer broke the silence.

"You're quite a marksman with that kickball, aren't you young fellow," Mr. Picklehoffer hollered at Rocco.

"Uh, uh, what happened, Sir?" Rocco stammered.

"Don't play dumb with me, boy!" Mr. Picklehoffer warned. "You just get down off your perch and get into my office this moment." Rocco just stood there trying to sort out what happened.

"Well, get!" the angry principal commanded. Rocco did. He moved so fast, however, he almost lost his balance. Only his arms that he frantically waved, circled and flapped, kept him from losing his balance. By now, practically the whole school population was viewing this spectacular event. They all went "ooh" when it looked like Rocco might do a swan dive smack onto the blacktop far below.

On the way into the building Mr. Picklehoffer had learned through the chattering students, that the ball got stuck on the roof. He would get the rest of the story from Rocco if he had to take it out of his hide.

Scott turned to Greg, "Boy, you really fixed Rocco this time. Nice going!"

"Yeah," a couple other players complained, "We can't even finish our game now that Rocco's gone."

The bell rang and everybody lined up. Greg welcomed the sound of the bell. If not for the timely recess bell, he thought he might be hanged by his heels, as for some kind of pinata celebration. Upon entering the classroom, the students were unusually quiet. They were all waiting to see if Rocco was around - or even alive. Of course, Rocco was not with his classmates at this time because he was being grilled by Mr. Picklehoffer in his office.

In the office, Mr. Picklehoffer scowled at Rocco and angrily asked, "Do you expect me to believe that you, up there on that roof, whooping and beating on your chest, have no clue as to how that ball got unstuck, and just *happened* to land on my head - twice!"

Rocco, in his most mannerly voice said, "Mr. Picklehoffer Sir, I have no idea how that ball got loose and found your head. Maybe the wind blew it off."

An increasingly frustrated Mr. Picklehoffer thrust his arm straight out toward the window and pointed to the flag. He growled, "Look at that flag. It hangs there as limp as a wet dishrag. Not one thread of that flag is moving. And you're telling me it's windy enough to blow that ball off the roof. You've told me some whoppers, Rocco Hardknuckle, but this story of yours today takes first prize."

After awhile Mr. Picklehoffer finally appeared in the doorway of the classroom. He said something about needing information. He tried to appear calm, but the tight muscles in his red face foretold of an explosion on hold. Particularly, he wanted to know the identity of the *last* person to touch the kickball before it plunked into the center of his head. Saying each word slowly but firmly, Mr. Picklehoffer asked, "Now, *who* was the last person to touch that ball?" He stood there, eyeing the class like a person who was determined to make somebody pay for a dark and evil deed.

Greg thought he might as well get it over with and tell the story. After all, it *was* an accident. He raised his hand. "Mr. Picklehoffer, my foot was the last thing to touch that ball." He then volunteered the whole story of how he kicked the high foul ball, and how it got stuck on the roof, and how he knocked it down with the softball. At that point, Mr. Picklehoffer interrupted him and informed him that he *knew* the rest of the story. He then called out in the hall for

Rocco to come in.

"Well, Rocco, you were right about one thing. You didn't throw the ball at me. But I still think there's a lesson for you in all of this. A fellow classmate of yours got the ball down *without* breaking school rules and *without* taking dangerous chances and *without* setting a bad example for the small children on the playground. Now, Rocco, guess how he got it down?" Mr. Picklehoffer asked.

Rocco was puzzled because he still didn't know how the ball got down.

"Well, Rocco - guess!" Mr. Picklehoffer commanded.

"Uh, uh...someone threw a ball at it and knocked it loose," he replied.

"You're right, Rocco! Now isn't that a much better way of handling the problem rather than breaking the rules and taking dangerous chances as you did?"

"Yes, Sir," Rocco replied obediently. He did not like being scolded in front of the class, but he had no choice than to grit his teeth and put up with it.

The principal continued, "Now, can you guess which one of your classmates had such a fine accurate throwing arm, *and* the good common sense to get the ball down in a safe manner?"

Rocco wanted the spotlight off him badly. He shrugged his shoulders, shook his head, and mumbled, "I dunno."

"Why," extending his arm toward Greg, "It's your friend, Greg Smith, right here in this very room. Greg, I hope you can teach Rocco a lesson or two on safety and common sense."

Now it was Greg's turn to hide. Why did Mr. Picklehoffer ever build *him* up at the expense of Rocco? Greg thought this would be the last straw as far as Rocco was concerned. Greg would be atop Rocco's enemies' list forever. When the principal had completed his little speech, Greg glanced very briefly at Rocco. He was staring daggers at Greg. If looks could kill, Greg would be headed for an early grave. The principal went on talking, but Greg did not hear a word of it. He was too busy gazing out the window, trying to avoid Rocco's piercing glare.

Chapter 19

Greg did not have to worry about getting clobbered on the way home because Rocco had to stay after school. Rocco also had to write a 500 word essay on the topic of safety. Greg wasn't sure Rocco knew 500 words.

Greg walked part way home with two boys from his class. One of the boys, Poker, was the first kid he'd met at Lincoln. He remembered how Poker asked him to play catch at recess right after his first "run in" with Rocco. Greg also recalled he warned him about how tough Rocco was.

"Greg, I've got to hand it to you," Poker said, with a touch of admiration, "You get into, and out of, more scrapes with Rocco than anybody I know. I really don't know how you do it."

"You know, Poker," Greg answered, "nobody wants to make peace with Rocco more than I do, but he always seems to be there. It's like - we just keep bumping into each other. Take today, for example. How was I to know he would get up on the roof to get the ball. How did I know Mr. Picklehoffer was going to come out nosing around just in time to get bonked on the head with the ball. But last of all, how did I know crazy Rocco was going to stand up there, and thump on his chest, and holler out a crazy Tarzan hoot. That's all *his* doing, not mine."

"Yeah, that all makes sense to *me*, but I'll bet Rocco doesn't see it that way," said Poker. "It was you who kicked the ball up on the roof even if it wasn't on purpose. It was you who knocked the ball off the roof so it smacked old Picklehoffer on the bean."

Greg had to admit to himself that Poker was probably right. He hoped Mother would be home and that she would ask him if anything interesting happened at school today. Would he have a story! He would always wait for Mother to ask, however. Greg was like that.

He went in the house, up the stairs, and threw his books on the bed. He quickly went back outside to the victory garden. He thought he was doing a good job of weeding and Grandpa Henry even told him so. He was eager to tell of his adventure in school but had seen no one yet. It was a funny story and he thought dinnertime the best place to tell it. That way everyone would hear it at the same time. While he weeded, he practiced just how he would tell it. He could hardly wait for dinner.

When his mother got home from work, Grandma called Grandpa to come in from the garage where he had been working. All sat down for dinner. When Grandma brought in a luscious smelling pot roast everyone was surprised. Meat, along with many other items, were rationed and when you bought something that was rationed, you not only gave the clerk the money, but also a certain amount of ration stamps. Rationing was a way to make sure everyone got enough of the items that were scarce. Buying more than what you need and stashing goods or food away was call "hoarding" and was considered unpatriotic. Gasoline, butter, flour, canned goods, meat, cheese, sugar, lard, coffee, rubber, were some of the items that were rationed.

"Wow," Mother exclaimed, "how did you ever get this delicious looking pot roast?"

"Well, I've just been saving up stamps," said Grandma. "Notice, we've not had much meat for awhile, so *enjoy*."

And everyone did. After the first flurry of dish passing, and first bites of the delicious meal, things settled down.

"Well Greg," mother asked, "did you learn anything in school today?" It was a question Mother often asked. Sometimes Greg could not think of an answer. But this time was different!

Greg thought the timing for telling his story was perfect. *Today*, he had a great story to unload.

He began, "Today I learned not to be a big loud-mouthed showoff like *Rocco*!"

Greg had told his mother a little bit about Rocco but his grandparents had not been "introduced" to him yet.

After a short description of Rocco and his bullying ways, Greg told them of the day's events. He began with him kicking the ball on the school roof and it getting stuck. Then he told of Rocco climbing onto the roof, and whooping and hollering like Tarzan, and Mr. Picklehoffer getting bonked on the noggin so hard his hat came down over his ears. They all had a good laugh and Greg was pleased.

Grandma said, "That's one of the funniest stories I've ever heard." Then she smiled and said, "This guy Rocco must have one giant-sized ego."

Greg looked puzzled and asked, "What do you mean?"

Grandma replied, "Ego is what you think of yourself. And it's good to think well of yourself. But people who think *too* much of themselves are said to have big egos. You know, they're always bragging themselves up and showing off. That kind of stuff."

Greg gave Grandma a "Yes-nod," and said, "Man, that's Rocco all right!"

Grandpa Henry said, "Well Son, when you think about it, maybe *everybody* has a big ego, but some just hide it better than others."

Mother said, "Yes that's a very funny story, but a guy like Rocco will want to settle the score with you. Then what?"

Greg said, "I don't know *what*." Greg had answered truthfully, because he did not know what Rocco would do, *and* he did not know how he would respond to whatever Rocco did. He was certain, however, that Rocco would do *something* to get even.

He tried to put it out of his mind but he could not. Thoughts about the next day were with him all evening.

He need not have worried however, because Rocco did not come to school. He was also absent the next day. On the third day following the Tarzan incident Rocco returned to school. Greg was concerned about his return, but he totally ignored Greg. It was as if nothing had happened. The remainder of the week passed by peacefully.

Chapter 20

Monday morning Greg decided to ride his precious "new" bike to school. He had been taking very good care of it and up till now only rode it around the neighborhood. He had not taken it to school for fear of something bad would happen to it. Despite his problems with Rocco, he felt more comfortable in the school now. Today, he decided he would ride it to school.

After eating breakfast with his grandparents, Grandma said, "Do you suppose you could help Grandpa and me haul some junk up from the basement? The city is collecting junk metal again for another scrap drive."

Greg said, "Sure, I'll come right home."

Grandma said, "You know, the government melts all that scrap down and then turns it into war material."

"Yeah," Greg replied. "Our teacher was just talking about that a few days ago. She said an old lawnmower could be turned into three, six inch shells. A steam iron could be turned into thirty hand grenades."

Grandpa Henry said, "I hope you don't have any more problems with Rocco today. Maybe he won't want to get into anymore trouble after that 'Tarzan' thing. Boy, that was funny!"

He said goodbye to his grandparents and thought it was strange not saying goodbye to his mother. Mother had finally gotten her call to come to work at the Happy Toy Co. and had to be there well before Greg's school time.

As he rode along, thoughts of Rocco came to mind. Each thought began with the words "What if..." What if *this* would happen, what it *that* would happen. Oh! Oh! What if Rocco was *really* barreling at you about a hundred miles an hour on his bike. And this was *not* some dream floating around in your brain. This *was* Rocco! He was all bent over, his chin 3 inches above his handlebars and pedaling so fast his feet were just a blur. Rocco and his bike were coming on like a missile and aimed right at Greg. Greg slowed down waiting for a possible crash. But no! At the very last second Rocco hit the brakes and came to a screeching, sliding, halt, right in front of him.

He looked Greg up and down and said, "Well now, I didn't know my little nuisance friend had a bike. Maybe after school we can get together and have a 'dog fight.' You know, our bikes can be fighter planes, just like in the war. I'll be a real American pilot and you can be some dirty ol' Nazi pilot. Man I'll mow you down so fast you won't even know what hit you."

Not waiting for an answer, Rocco wheeled his bike around and took off.

"Well shoot," Greg grumbled to himself, "there goes my day. I'll have to use every minute trying to figure out a safe way home."

Several times during class, Greg was caught off guard by questions from Miss Johnson and also from his classmates. His mind would slip back and forth, from class activities, to how he would get home safely.

Throughout the day Rocco would occasionally look back over his shoulder and smile at Greg. It was not a friendly smile, but more of an *I'm-gonna-gitcha* smile. Greg was hoping with all his might Rocco would screw up and have to stay after school.

It didn't happen. As soon as Miss Johnson dismissed the class, Rocco was gone. Seeing this, Greg decided to stay a few minutes and clean out his desk. This would give Rocco time to leave the schoolyard. Just maybe, Greg thought, Rocco would forget about his promise to "shoot him down."

That didn't happen. When Greg left the building he saw Rocco riding around in tight circles on the playground. The school rules were that you get your bike from the rack and ride straight off the playground. But school rules never bothered Rocco. Round and round the playground he rode, in tight little circles and figure eights.

Greg couldn't see any other option open to him other than to get on his bike, and start riding home. Whatever happens happens and he will just have to deal with it. He didn't look right or left but went straight to the bike rack. He took the bike out of the rack and pedaled off. Once on the bike, he took a quick look to see if Rocco was around. His enemy had disappeared.

He decided to take a shortcut through an empty parking lot. He was almost through it, when a figure flew out from a cluster of trees by the side of the lot. It was Rocco!

Playing a fighter pilot role, Rocco rode straight at Greg and made machine gun noises - "rat-a-tat-tat, rat-a-tat-tat." At the very last second before the bikes would collide, Rocco turned away. He made a wide circle and again came straight at Greg. Greg swerved to avoid a terrible crash.

Many students had stopped on their way home to watch. Rocco had put the word out that there would be some "excitement" after school.

Greg decided to ride fast and get off the lot and onto the street. Halfway to the exit Rocco made another pass at him, narrowly missing the front wheel of Greg's bike. Greg nearly lost his balance but recovered and sped on.

Rocco yelled at Greg, "Missed you again, you sorry stinkin' Nazi, but I'll get you next time." By the time Rocco came out of his turn he was well behind Greg. Rocco's powerful legs thrust his bike forward much faster than Greg, however. He was rapidly gaining on Greg and Greg knew this.

Rocco had a wild and daring idea. When he drew even with Greg he would leap from his bike onto Greg's back, just like they do in cowboy movies. It would mean a brutal spill on the cement for the both of them, but man he thought, the crowd would go crazy!

Greg was bearing down on the exit, with Rocco now only a few yards behind him. Just before the exit there were two barricades about 3 feet apart, blocking off an area of newly laid cement. Was it dry enough to ride over? Greg didn't think so and swerved around the area at the last second.

Rocco did not! He saw an opportunity to catch Greg by taking a shortcut through the barricades and riding over the cement. He had a devilish smile on his face at the thought of finally catching Greg. He would take the chance. Surely the cement was dry enough by now to support his bike.

Rocco hollered at Greg, "I gotcha now you lousy little Nazi skunk."

Shirttail flying in the wind, Rocco stood up and pedaled to gain even more speed. He shot through the gap in the barricades at full speed. There was a board laying on the pavement and when the bike hit it, Rocco jerked upward on the handlebars and the bike lifted gracefully into the air. It was a magnificent sight: a smiling, confident Rocco, hunched over his handlebars, gliding through the air, and about to catch his elusive prey.

When the front wheel of the bike came down, however, it did not touch down on solid cement. Instead, it came down with a loud, "Plop," in gooey wet cement. The front wheel rolled not more than 6 inches and suddenly stopped. Immediately the back wheel hit the goop with another loud plop.

Rocco had been going so fast and stopped so suddenly, his rear end started to carry over the handlebars. And it kept rising until he was nearly doing a handstand. He desperately held on to the handlebars as he peered down in shock at the wet muck waiting to claim him. But gravity did its job and pulled him back onto his bike seat with a loud thud.

All the while the spectators were echoing out "Ooos" and "Ahs," as though they were watching a fireworks display. For a second after Rocco hit the seat, the bike and rider remained upright like a statue. Then Rocco and the bike slowly began to lean to one side, as a huge tree falls after it has been cut. One of the onlookers even hollered, "Timberrr!"

Coming out of his state of shock, Rocco tried to put his leg out to keep from falling. He could not! His pant leg was caught in the bike chain. Rocco and his bike, together as one, fell sideways into the wet, white, slop. This was *not* the "excitement" that Rocco had planned for his classmates to see!

Rocco and his bike lay quietly in the cement. The crowd was silent. All action came to an abrupt stop. Then, very slowly, Rocco began to move. Although he was lying flat in the cement, he was still in his riding position, so he had to struggle to free his legs from the bike. He wallered around in the muck and was finally able to get on his hands and knees. By now, the wet, white cement dripped and drooped from his entire body.

When the crowd realized Rocco was okay, they began to look at each other and smile, shaking their heads in disbelief at the comical scene. Their smiles quickly turned to outright laughter as they watched Rocco sliding around in the slippery slop.

One student hollered, "I just got here Rocco. Want to show me how you did that again?"

Another shouted, "Throw him a life preserver."

A girl, laughing so hard she was bent over, was able to catch enough breath to answer, "Life preserver? What he needs is a trowel!"

Someone waved his arms trying to get the crowd's attention and said, "Hey, listen up, when he dries we can haul him up to the park and put him with the other statues."

"Yeah, right next to that Civil War cannon," someone said.

"Well," a boy chuckled. "At least he's all white so the pigeon poop won't show so bad."

All the while Rocco was bent over trying to retrieve his bike. This was no easy task. The cement was heavy and did not want to give up the bike. But after much huffing and puffing he managed to raise it to his side.

He very carefully began walking, not wanting to lose his balance. Each step made a "plop" sound. Plop, plop, plop echoed over the scene as Rocco trudged toward the edge of the parking lot. He walked cautiously, but with purpose and determination.

The sight of this dripping white, ghostly figure slowly stepping out of the muck, looked unreal. He looked like an evil, non-human character from some sci-fi horror movie, stalking out of an unearthly, all-white swamp.

Rocco finally extracted himself from the cement. On solid ground at last, he turned and faced the crowd of kids, who by the way, were all howling with laughter. Rocco was determined not to be defeated by this totally embarrassing event.

With a mighty thrust, he raised the bicycle above his head. It looked as though he was trying to say something but couldn't get the words out. Then, wrinkling his nose and making a sour face, he spat out a frightful wad of cement. Clearing his throat he shouted, "I, Super Hero Cement Man will return to fight for justice and the American way, another day!"

Not one second after he ended this grand proclamation, great globs of wet cement dropped from his bike. Most of this slimy ooze landed squarely on his head where it rolled from his ears, dripped from his nose, and dribbled off his chin.

The crowd was going crazy. However, throughout all this, Rocco defiantly held the bike high over his head. As a final show of swagger, he let go of the bike with one arm and made a muscle of it. Now, holding the bike with only one arm, he capped off this feat with another of his mighty Tarzan yells, "Ow-ee-ow, ow-ee-ow!" With his free arm he began doing Tarzan thumps on his chest. Drops of cement sprayed from his soaked shirt with every thump.

Looking over his shoulder, Greg had seen Rocco do his spectacular leap, and following collapse, into the cement. He had pedaled a short distance more, stopped his bike, and turned around to see Rocco's "Cement Man" act.

Greg hated to admit it but he felt a touch of admiration for Rocco. Here Rocco is, totally humiliated, but he turns around and makes a joke out of it. Then he remembered what Grandpa Henry once said: "Any man who can laugh at himself, ain't *all* bad." Was there hope for Rocco, he wondered?

Chapter 21

Greg returned home and asked Grandma what junk she wanted hauled out of the basement for the scrap drive.

Grandma said, "Greg honey, it's all piled up at the foot of the basement stairs. Just put it out by the curb and the city workers will pick it up tomorrow."

Then Grandma's expression turned very thoughtful and she said, "Greg, all that metal is going to be melted down and turned into something else. I just can't help but wonder what it will be. And then, where in the world will it end up?"

Greg said, "I hope it's turned into something like tanks, bombs, guns, ammo, anything that will help win this war so Dad can get home. Everyday I wonder what he's doing, like right now, this very minute, what you suppose he's doing?"

Grandma shook her head in agreement and said, "I'll bet he wonders the exact same thing about you and your mother."

After Greg hauled up the junk from the basement Grandma said, "Oh Greg, there's one more thing. I ran out of coffee. Molly always has some extra because she only drinks a small cup a day. She and I are always borrowing and trading those rationed items. So could you run over there and ask her if she could spare a bit of coffee?"

As Greg stepped outside, he noticed what looked like Miss Johnson's 1937 Ford parked in front of Mrs. Sutter's home. That was strange he thought. He loved her car with its pointed, stream-lined grill. He was about to ring the doorbell when the door opened. It was Miss Johnson, who appeared to be just leaving. Each face showed surprise in seeing the other.

Miss Johnson spoke first, "Oh Greg! How nice to see you. What brings you to Mrs. Sutter's house?"

Greg replied, "I live across the street with my mom, and Grandpa and Grandma Olson. Grandma sent me over to see if Mrs. Sutter had some coffee. I guess we're out."

Greg, who was still puzzled at seeing his teacher, asked, "Do you know Mrs. Sutter?"

Miss Johnson answered, "I sure do. I grew up in this neighbor-hood and I've known her for a long time. As a matter of fact, I saw you riding home from school today on a bike that looked awfully familiar. It belonged to Steve, that is Mrs. Sutter's son. Right?"

"You're right," replied Greg.

Miss Johnson continued, "Well it might be hard to believe, but I've even ridden that bike. One summer afternoon a bunch of us kids were just messing around here in her yard. Mrs. Sutter had just given us some lemonade and cookies. She was always doing nice things like that for us kids. I was in fourth grade and Steve was in sixth grade. I told Steve I'd like to try and ride his bike and he said the bike is too big for a little girl to ride. I told him I was no little girl."

He said, "Okay smarty, you try and ride it, but don't go blaming me if you break your neck."

Miss Johnson continued, "So I was able to get on it, but I could barely reach the pedals. I came to the end of the sidewalk and couldn't brake it. I rolled off the curbing, lost my balance, and landed on the street. I skinned my knee and elbow so badly they bled. It also put a dent in the front fender of his bike."

Then Miss Johnson laughed and said, "That's not all. Steve's mom happened to see the accident and she really got angry at Steve for letting me ride his bike! Then she invited me in and took care of my wounds. Steve was so mad at me, he ignored me for weeks. And, I steered clear of him!"

"Well, I've got to run now," Miss Johnson said. "Hope I didn't bore you with my childhood story."

"No, you didn't," Greg replied.

Greg continued on with his errand and knocked on Mrs. Sutter's door. She invited him in and yes, she did have extra coffee for Greg's grandmother.

While waiting, he took a long look at the picture of Capt. Sutter again. He was wearing a leather flight jacket and standing in front of the big B17 bomber. There was the name "Molly's Angel" painted in big letters below the cockpit where the pilot sat.

At the movies they always showed what was called "newsreels." They were a series of brief scenes of what was going on in the world. They would usually show some war scenes and he remembered once seeing film taken from a U.S. bomber during a bombing raid. Puffs of black smoke covered the sky where antiaircraft shells exploded. How could anyone ever fly through that, he wondered. After the bombers were out of reach of the antiaircraft guns, Nazi fighter planes would swoop out from the clouds and try to riddle the bombers to the ground. He thought of what Mrs. Sutter said, and her questions about where her son was, and what he might be doing at this very moment. And now he wondered the same about his father.

Concerns of what would happen tomorrow with Rocco soon crowded out everything else. Rocco could not possibly think it was his fault he wound up wearing a suit of wet cement. However, to Rocco, maybe the truth of the situation was not as important as protecting his ego. Be they real reasons, or merely lame excuses, the list of issues Rocco has against him keeps piling up: the stack of books episode, the yo-yo scene, the "Leaping Linda" basketball defeat, the Tarzan-on-the-roof disaster, and now the "Cement Man" embarrassment.

As concerned as Greg was about the cement incident, he couldn't help but smile at the thought of all that gooey cement dripping off Rocco's ears, nose and chin. He would have to stay out of his way for quite awhile. On the other hand he couldn't just disappear. Stressful times like these made him wish to return to Riverside.

The next morning Greg was not sure whether he should ride his bike to school. He rode it yesterday with horrible results. Greg stood there just staring at it trying to make up his mind. It was then he noticed a slight wrinkle on the bottom of the front fender. It looked rough and a bit scratched. There was also a slight crease where the edge of the metal had been bent. It looked to Greg as though some- one tried to straighten it but the flaw was still visible. Was this the result of the accident Miss Johnson had told him about?

He tried to imagine what the scene was like: the sharp words between them, Steve's anger at the young Miss Johnson, the bloody knee and elbow. It was probably a real big deal then, but now it's just a funny story. He wondered what Miss Johnson and Captain Sutter looked like as youngsters. And would he remember scenes from his own days growing up as did Miss Johnson?

He shook himself back to reality. Too late now to walk. He had to ride his bike and hope things would turn out better today.

All the kids were in line waiting to be called into the build- ing. While he was running to get in line, he looked for Rocco. The second Greg saw him, Rocco turned and saw Greg. Their eyes met. Rocco was not smiling. Fortunately, Rocco did not have his homework done and he had to stay in at recess to complete it. On the playground a circle of boys called to Greg to come over. They were all talking about Rocco the "Cement Spook" as one boy had dubbed him.

The same boy asked Greg, "Wasn't that the funniest thing you ever saw in your entire life?"

Greg did not want to say anything for fear that it would get back to Rocco. So he only shrugged his shoulders and said, "Well, I hope he didn't get hurt."

He wanted no more questions and said, "I'm going over and shoot baskets. Anybody want to come?" The rest of the day was uneventful. He and Rocco never crossed paths and Rocco had schoolwork to complete after school.

Chapter 22

The week passed by in a hurry. Rocco did not speak once to him but everything else went pretty well. He received two A's in tests. His mother told him he could clean out the old aquarium and get some new fish. And finally, Sue had been extra nice to him the past few days. So everything considered, it had been a good week.

Twice he hiked out to his tree by the bend in the creek. He was almost hoping that Sue would see him and come out to talk. However, she did not. He was not too disappointed though because he had a chance to sit there alone, and to think. And although Sue *was* very easy to talk to, it was still much easier talking to boys. Talking to boys took much less energy.

He was on his third trip to the tree this week. The leaves of the tree had changed color now. They were a dark chestnut brown. It always seemed strange to him that a tree sticking out of the creek bank at such an odd angle could be alive. Seeing the leaves beginning to turn gave him an eerie feeling. It was as if something that was supposed to be dead wouldn't die, no matter what.

He had taken a pocketful of rocks up in the branches of the tree so that he could bomb floating leaves as they gently drifted by. Plunk, plunk, plunk. He lobbed three of them at an oak leaf bobbing along near the shore. As the rocks hit the water, the "plunk" sound made a faint echo. He tired of this quickly and decided to change targets. He aimed at three leaves bunched together, but at a distance. He let all of his fist full of rocks go at the same time. There was a short spattering sound as the rocks pelted the water. He loved that sound. The make-believe missiles did not strike their target and the leaves were free to go on their course.

At that instant, he heard footsteps coming out of the woods. He smiled to himself because he was confident it was Sue. His heart quickened as he thought of what he would say to her. He wanted to appear cool and not too eager, so he didn't turn around to look. Next, he heard footsteps climbing up the bark of the tree. He thought Sue should have hollered some kind of greeting to him by now. Suddenly, he felt an urgent need to turn around and know who was there. He did. The shock of the discovery nearly knocked him off his perch and into the water. It was Rocco!

"Oh, uh, hi!" Greg was startled and he knew it showed on his face. "What are you doing here?" Greg went on.

"Watcha mean, Skunk, this tree's always been my place. Got my initials in it right over there," he replied gruffly. He continued to climb out to where Greg sat, talking all the while. "You know, you and I got a lot of unfinished business to settle. Right up here in this tree might be a good place to get it squared away. What ya say, Skunk?"

Greg was not usually slow with words, but this time not one word came into his head. He didn't know what Rocco had in mind, perhaps talk, perhaps fight. Greg thought he might as well hope for the best and expect to talk. He was already seated, but turned around and made himself more comfortable by leaning against a branch. Not only was the position more comfortable, but it would show Rocco that he was relaxed and was not thinking about fighting. Meanwhile, Rocco had joined him and sat straddling the tree trunk.

Finally, Greg asked, "What's on your mind?" It was not an honest question. Greg *did* know what was on Rocco's mind. What he *didn't* know was how Rocco planned to settle their dispute.

They were sitting there eye to eye with Rocco staring coldly at Greg. "You think about it, Skunk. Just think about it," he said.

At last some words, phrases, and ideas started floating to the surface of Greg's mind. "Okay, let me guess. You think I get in your way a lot. Maybe you're mad because old Mr. Picklehoffer thought you threw the ball at him and you got all that punishment for being on the roof. Maybe you think it's my fault because you fell in the cement."

"Yeah," Rocco growled. "All that and more. Skunk, let me tell you something. Every time I get around you, something bad happens to me. But I'm not going to even the score here. I want a crowd to be watching, a really *big* crowd. Just know Skunk, it's on its way."

Suddenly Rocco's attention was turned away from Greg. "Look!" he said in a quick, excited voice. He pointed to the water below. Several feet from shore there was a small head sticking out of the water. "I think it's a turtle. I think if we're careful, we could catch it."

Was this Tubby, the same turtle he had hit with a rock? Greg thought that there was a good chance it was. Greg had never caught a turtle before and for *sure* he didn't want to catch this one.

"Yeah," Greg said, "I've seen that turtle before. I called it Tubby." Greg was about to tell Rocco of accidently hitting Tubby with a rock. But Rocco didn't give him a chance.

Rocco interrupted, "You mean you gave that low life reptile a name?" Then his voice dripped with pretended sympathy and tenderness and he said, "Oh, ain't that sweet."

Rocco grinned at Greg and went on, "Skunk, you know what? I just think I'll catch ol' Tubby here and ask him a few questions.

Maybe I'll ask him how he likes his new name. Maybe I can teach him how to sit up and rollover. Or, maybe he could go fetch me a minnow or something like that."

Rocco scrambled down the tree to the creek bank, all the while keeping a steady eye on the turtle. He was not watching where he was going and nearly tripped and fell over a tree branch. When he reached the ground he stayed low, behind some bushes close to the tree. The turtle was about 20 feet away and was approaching the creek bank. There was a sandy stretch of shoreline where the turtle plodded out of the creek and onto the sand. One of the turtle's back legs was useless. It was limp and he dragged it behind him. This *had* to be Tubby Turtle Greg thought. And yes, without a doubt, the rock he threw had lamed the unfortunate creature.

When Tubby was about 5 feet onto the sand, Rocco raced over and blocked the turtle's path back to the water. Sensing danger, the turtle turned back toward the creek, only to find his escape route blocked. The turtle picked up his three clumsy feet and with added effort, tried to go around him. His plodding efforts were futile, however. The towering figure above him bent over and swooped him up.

"I've got it! I've got it!" he shouted. He turned toward Greg and held the helpless turtle high above his head with both hands. He looked like an athlete who had just won a trophy and was showing it off to his fans.

It was not a pretty turtle. It had a blackish shell that was coated with a touch of green slime.

"You better watch it, Rocco," Greg warned. "That looks like a genuine snapping turtle to me."

"See, that's the way it is with you, Skunk," Rocco answered. "I can't do anything but what you get in the way. Here I make a big catch and you don't even congratulate me. Instead, you give me this big warning about something you know nothing about."

"I was just trying to help. I wouldn't want to see you get a good finger all torn up," Greg replied. Greg continued on, "But see, that's the way it is with *you*, Rocco. You're always thinking I want bad things to happen to you, or that I want to put you down. All I care to do is get along and not be hassled. That's all!"

Rocco shot back, "Skunk, even if what you say is true, it doesn't matter. You are just plain bad luck for me. Nothing you can do is going to change that."

Rocco carefully placed the captive turtle belly down in the sand. He was a good jailer and was careful not to let him escape. Every time the turtle moved one way, he would quickly block his path. Mostly, however, the turtle just sat there waiting for his freedom to be returned. But it was not to be. Not with "Rocco the Jailer" in control. The turtle made another desperate rush in an effort to get free, but again Rocco jumped in front of him.

"Oh, no you don't mister slow guy," he warned. "If you're going to get tricky with me, I'll fix you up good." And after that threat, he flipped the turtle on his back. The turtle's three working legs churned away in a slow, steady rhythm, but only pushed air. Tubby Turtle strained first one way and then the other. His eyes appeared very large. The poor creature's world was suddenly turned upside down. His frantic movements showed his fear.

Greg was still perched in the tree, but he was no longer in his relaxed position. Rocco's tormenting of the turtle really bothered him. He was worried about how far he would go with his teasing. Greg still said nothing. Next, Rocco grabbed a fistful of sand, stood over the turtle and allowed the sand to slowly stream onto the bottom side of the turtle's shell.

"I wonder if he could ever turn himself over?" Rocco asked the question as if he might be talking to himself. "I'll bet he can't if he's buried," he continued. He picked up two more fistfuls of sand and allowed two more fine streams to pelt the turtle's underbelly.

Turning to Greg, he asked, "What ya say, Skunk? You think this old guy could ever flip himself over?" He was determined to find out whether Greg had any sympathy for his new captive.

"I don't know," Greg answered. Another stream of sand was now pouring over the turtle's belly. Greg did not wish to give Rocco a signal it was bothering him for fear he would do even more. Rocco was obviously hassling the turtle to irritate he, Greg.

Now with both hands cupped, Rocco scooped up several more handfuls of sand and dumped them on the turtle. When the last grain of sand had hit the pile, only the turtle's head was showing. Rocco looked up at Greg to see what his reaction would be. Greg remained silent.

Rocco smiled and said, "Skunk, what if I'd just leave this ugly thing here with his ugly head sticking out? Wonder how long it would take before the ants would find it and start chomping away on it. What's your guess, Skunk? A day? Two days? Bad way to go huh? Wouldn't want *my* head sticking out down there with a couple a hundred ants chewing away on it."

Greg said nothing.

"Well," Rocco said, "I wouldn't do that. That'd be cruel. I'm not cruel. I'm just a little ornery that's all."

Rocco decided to begin all over again. He lifted the turtle from the sand and set him right side up. The turtle limped toward the water, the injured leg dragging behind him. He scooped up two handfuls of sand and slowly poured it on the creature's head. The turtle's pace quickened as it crawled desperately toward the creek.

Then, putting his toe under the turtle's shell, he flipped the struggling turtle over once more. "I got you again old man," Rocco said, and then gave his long, evil sounding, "The Shadow," laugh.

That was the last straw, Greg thought. He had to do something. He didn't know what, but he just had to do *something*!

Greg began climbing out of the tree. Seeing this, Rocco hollered up to him, "Hey man, coming down to get in on the fun?"

Fun, Greg thought, he knew Rocco was getting to him with that turtle. Rocco was waiting for him to blow his cool. Greg did not answer him. He climbed out of the tree and went to where he was tormenting the turtle.

Rocco began pouring sand on the bottom side of the turtle again. He said, "I'm really going to bury him this time. Yeah, a real groovy grave."

Greg did not know where to begin in his attempt to free the turtle. One thought running through his mind was that he could just pick it up and slip it into the water. He could do it quickly so Rocco would not know what was happening. That was probably the surest and quickest way to get it done. But that wouldn't set well with Rocco, for sure. It would make the hard feelings between them much worse. There had to be a better way, he thought.

Greg finally decided to play on his sympathy. Greg thought if Rocco had any sympathy at all, it would be measured in ounces not pounds. But he would try anyway. He began his plan by saying, "I'll bet that poor crippled turtle is wondering whether he'll ever see the bottom of that creek again."

"Skunk, that turtle isn't wondering about anything," he replied. "I should have known you'd be on the turtle's side," he moaned while continuing to rain sand on the upside-down turtle. "Do you think this dumb turtle is dreaming about anything? He probably can't get one picture in that peanut-sized brain of his."

"How do you know," Greg answered. "You ever been a turtle?"

Rocco ignored Greg's question and said, "If I'd let 'em go, he'd find his creek bottom okay, but only because of his instincts." Continuing his "turtle speech" he said, "Turtles just do whatever Mr. Instinct tells them to do. Turtles don't hurt and they don't even think," Rocco protested. "They just do."

Greg realized his plan to arouse Rocco's sympathy was going nowhere. He would try another tactic.

Greg asked, "Rocco, have you ever asked yourself *why* you get pleasure out of seeing a helpless animal like this struggle to get free?"

Rocco silently stared at the turtle and watched the thin stream of sand bounce off his underbelly.

Greg decided to press him further for an answer. "Seriously Rocco, what's the pleasure you get out of watching a creature suffer?"

Rocco remained silent. There was no movement in his face, no sign of any sort of emotion. He simply stood there, like a statue. The only movement was the narrow stream of sand still striking the turtle.

The last bit of sand bounced off the turtle. Rocco's eyes remained fixed on his captive. At this moment, Greg wondered if his words had touched a part of Rocco that had some sense of feeling. Had he planted some kind of "goodness seed" in Rocco's brain that might eventually take root and grow?

Then Rocco shook his head as if coming out of a trance. He acted as if freed from some momentary brush with his conscience. He scooped up the turtle with both hands. He flipped it right side up and balanced it on one hand. He held it shoulder high, as a waiter would carrying a tray of food.

Greg said, "Boy Rocco, I'd be careful with that old guy. Like I said, I think he could be a real snapper. And snappers love fingers."

"Skunk," he replied, "there you go again, flapping your tongue about something you know nothing about. You couldn't tell a snapping turtle from a giraffe."

The turtle's three good legs churned away at the air, and his head and neck strained one way and then another, as if in movement, there was hope.

Then Rocco held his index finger directly in front of the turtle and said, "Okay, Mr. Turtle, you can have one of my tasty fingers for lunch."

Tubby accepted Rocco's invitation. His strong jaws snapped onto Rocco's finger like a spring-loaded steel trap.

Rocco's eyes widened with surprise...then pain...then panic! He let go of the turtle immediately. The turtle's vise-like grip remained solidly clamped on his finger. He began shaking the turtle. Then he swung it around in the air. The creature held fast and the weight of the turtle made the pain much worse.

Rocco turned to Greg, tears now filling his eyes and pleaded, "Greg, *do* something. *Anything*! *Please?*"

Greg had never seen such a sight before in his life: a turtle hanging onto someone's finger, the victim overcome with pain and fear. He didn't know what to do.

Angry tears rolled down Rocco's face and he hollered at Greg, "Do *something*! *Please!*"

Greg had an idea. "Rocco," he said, "Try wading out in the creek, and very quietly put your hand way under the water. Maybe he'll think the battle is over and let go and swim away."

Without any hesitation, Rocco charged into the water. He submerged the turtle and his arm in about three feet of water.

Greg said, "Be still now. Don't move."

Rocco did exactly as he was told. He shut his eyes and gritted his teeth, trying his best to remain motionless and to *will* away the pain. In a minute Rocco felt the turtle's grip loosen. Seconds later, the turtle swam away to freedom. Rocco trudged out of the water looking like a dripping dishrag. He kneeled on the sandy shore staring at the raw, bleeding finger.

Greg didn't know what to say. Inside he was partly feeling sorry for Rocco, and partly laughing at his dumb mistake. And for sure, he was silently cheering the turtle. Greg finally sorted through his thinking. First aid seemed to be most important right now.

Greg warned Rocco, "You'd better get something on that finger. It could get infected. You need any help?"

Rocco did not reply, but hurriedly walked away. His jeans were soaked tight to his legs and his shoes squeaked with each step, as the water oozed out of his tennis shoes. In fact everything about him either drooped or dripped. In a matter of minutes, his whole character seemed transformed. He was no longer the bragging jailer of a tormented turtle. He was only a young boy plodding home, cold, wet, scared and scarred.

Chapter 23

Greg returned from the creek shortly before dinner. He did not know if he should tell about Tubby's lunching on Rocco's index finger. Mother asked the same old tired question, "What did you learn in school today, Greg?"

Greg answered, "Well, Miss Johnson wanted to know what we knew about the victory slogan. You know, the letter 'V' you see everywhere."

Then Mother asked, "And what *do* you know?"

"Well," Greg said, "of course everyone knows the 'V' stands for 'Victory.' But I didn't know there was a connection between the 'V' in the Morse Code and a famous symphony."

Grandpa Henry broke in, "Don't tell me Son, I learned the Morse Code in the navy. For the letter 'V' it is dot-dot-dot-dash. Right? But I wouldn't have a clue about that symphony stuff."

Greg had to pause and think about how to describe it. He said, "Beethoven's Fifth Symphony starts out like that," and he hummed, "da da da daaa." Then he said, "It repeats, only lower, 'da da da daaa."

"Oh, I get it," Grandma Henrietta said. "The short da's stand for the three dots and the long 'daaa' is the dash. How clever," she said, and hummed the notes as Greg had done.

Greg said, "You got it Grandma. And after that "da da da daaa" beginning, it just takes off with a flurry of other notes and gets really wild. You should hear it. But every once and awhile it comes back the way it started, da-da-da-daaa. I guess you'd say it's the theme that runs through the piece."

"Sure," Mother said. "In the movies when they cover the war in the newsreel they'll often begin with that same music da-da-da-daaa, da-da-da-daaa."

Then Greg continued, "And look at all the businesses that have 'victory' in their names, like downtown here we have a Victory Café."

Grandma Henrietta said, "Don't forget our 'Victory' gardens, and the 'Victory' sign," as she held up two fingers forming the "V."

Grandpa Henry said, "I think we've more than covered all that 'V' stuff. If I hear anymore of it I'm going to 'V' for *vomit*."

Grandma Henrietta said sternly, "Henry, that's not appropriate talk for dinner. I'm surprised at you."

Mother said, "I guess Grandpa isn't as *virtuous* as we thought."

Then they all began to get silly and start laughing.

Mother, hoping to have the final word said, "Let's all just shut up and eat our *victuals*!"

After the 'V for Victory' topic was finally put to rest, Greg decided to share the story about Tubby Turtle dining on Rocco's index finger.

Grandma Henrietta said, "From what you've said about that Rocco Hardknuckle character, he certainly got what he deserved. Too bad he didn't swallow up everything to the bully's elbow."

The next morning Greg looked all over the playground for Rocco but did not see him. Scott came over and said, "Hey man, where'd you get the bike? About the same as mine only a touch older. Good shape, where'd you get it?"

Greg replied, "A neighbor who lives across the street gave it to me for some chores I'll do for her. It was her son's. He's in England now flying a B17 bomber. Guess she figured he won't be needing it anymore."

"Have you seen Rocco?" Greg asked.

"Yeah, I stopped in for him on the way to school. Said he might not come today. He hurt his finger big time. He took the bandage off and showed me. It looked just *awful*. It's all bruised and swollen. And you know what? He wouldn't tell me what happened except that he got in a big fight with an animal he was trying to catch. Yeah, it attacked him. Wouldn't say what kind, or where, or nothing. Must a been some ferocious critter though, to tear up a finger like that."

Greg did not know what to say. Should he tell Scott that the so called "ferocious" critter was only a turtle who was trying to get away? Should he tell him Rocco had taunted the turtle without mercy? Should he tell him how Rocco stupidly put his finger in the turtle's face and invited him to chew on it?

Rocco's incomplete story could leave Scott with the picture of him facing down a growling wolverine or a bear! Greg considered whether to tell Scott the truth. It would surely get a big laugh. It was so funny it would go around the school like a firestorm. And Greg could be laughing right with them. But then there's the other side of it - the downside of telling it. Since he, Greg, was the only one there, Rocco would know who told. That was it. As funny as it was, Greg decided not to spread the story around. For a fleeting moment he thought maybe he could tell Scott, and tell him to keep it a secret. But then he thought of what Grandpa Henry once said, "Nobody ever tells somebody a secret." When he first heard it, he had to think about those words for awhile before he caught the meaning of the message.

Rocco did come to school that day, but late. He was very quiet and was wearing a big bandage on his finger. For the rest of the week Rocco seemed content to ignore Greg.

The following Monday morning after parking his bike in the rack, a voice behind him asked, "Been to the tree lately?"

It was Sue. Greg was surprised, but pleased she asked. "Yeah," he replied, "a couple of times. Didn't see you though."

"Well I've been there too. Actually, I was kind of looking for you," she said.

Greg was shocked. He tried to come up with a response. Anything! No words came out of his mouth. He just stood there staring at her.

Sue kept walking but turned her head back to him and said, "You know you *could* call me next time you go over there. It's the only 'Love' in the phone book." She said this with a slight smile. Greg thought if a smile could ever talk, *this* smile said; "I *really* want to talk to you." He would remember it forever. And her last name "Love." How uncommon! You could never forget a name like that.

He was startled back into reality when Scott and several other boys from his class passed by him. Scott said, "That Sue really likes you. Least that's what's going around."

Another boy in the group teased, "Gee, ain't that sweet?"

Another said, "I heard she thinks you're cute."

Someone else broke in and said, "Hey man, I wish Sue would think I'm cute. She's really neat!" He nodded over to where Sue and some girls were jumping rope and continued, "Good rope jumper too."

Other boys joined the group. Greg was still looking at her and watching her ponytail bounce along in rhythm to her rope jumping. What a great sight he thought!

Out of the corner of his eye he saw Rocco running toward the group. Here comes trouble he thought. However, if given a thousand guesses, he would never have predicted how the events would unfold that day.

Chapter 24

One boy announced Rocco's arrival, "Here comes Rocco, the Rock." Rocco barged into the group, clapping his hands, and generally interrupting all conversation. He began telling about a war movie he had seen recently. Greg's eyes kept bouncing back and forth between Rocco and Sue. He noticed that whenever Rocco said something he would wave his arms, point, move his head and continually pace around. It was as if he were talking with his entire body.

Greg's attention was still going back and forth between Sue and Rocco when he was jarred out of his thoughts by a sharp elbow to his ribs. It was Scott who asked, "Ain't that right, Greg?"

Greg had been watching Rocco, but not listening to him. He knew the subject of the war movie had passed by, but he didn't have a clue as to what they were talking about now. He decided to agree with Scott and hope the conversation would move on. "You're right Scott," Greg said.

Rocco looked sharply at Greg. It was clear he was not pleased by Greg's answer. Greg tried to recover, "I...I guess I missed the question," he stammered. "What was it you said?"

Another boy quickly spoke up, "Scott thinks Rocco is going to have to stay after school again today because he goofs around all the time and never gets his work done."

Rocco's eyes narrowed as he looked at Greg and said, "And you agreed with him, Skunk!"

It was something Scott and a couple of other buddies could say to Rocco. But not Greg!

He walked slowly over to Greg until he was nose-to-nose with him. With his fists tightly clenched he said, "It just wasn't my lucky day when you moved here, Skunk."

Scott interrupted and teased, "Oh c'mon, Rocco. You're just kidding us. You know darned well you love to stay in and help Teach with bulletin boards and all that decorating stuff."

Another of Rocco's friends kidded, "Why, we all know Rocco's the best paper cutter and paster in the room."

Scott continued, "And since you like to stay in and be Teach's little helper, Greg here should be your best friend. Smart as he is in getting you into trouble, you'll be able to spend loads of time practicing all that cutting and pasting. The Rock's getting better than the girls at it. Won't be long before we can put a pretty dress on him."

That was it! Rocco could take no more. He lit out after Scott and chased him around in a circle. Scott was too fast for him, however, so he gave up the chase. He began snarling at Scott pretending he was a dog.

"Dare you to come back here," Rocco taunted. Although he did not appear really angry, he was clearly embarrassed at the thought of Greg, this new kid, getting the best of him all the time. The words between Rocco and Scott had stopped and everything was suddenly still.

Rocco was back in the circle now and his eyes were fixed on Greg. "When I get out of school, I'm going to be a professional wrestler," he vowed. He crouched low, held his arms outstretched with the palms of his hands up. It was a typical wrestling position. He moved about the circle of boys pretending to be a tough looking wrestler. He growled as he moved about and beckoned with his hands for a challenger to come forth.

He was still kidding around and did not seem serious. The onlookers joined in the fun, laughing and teasing him. Scott was back in the circle again and shouted, "Hey, maybe you and the new kid could wrestle for the championship of the world."

Rocco threw his arms in the air and shouted, "Wow, that's a great idea. I can see it all now. Our name in lights in New York City, fearless Rocco "The Rock" Hardknuckle versus ... versus ... what's your real name again Skunk?"

"Greg ... Greg Smith," he answered in a halting voice. He was worried about how far Rocco would go with this wrestling act. His shaky voice gave away his concern about it.

"Aha! How could I ever forget an exciting name like that?" Rocco said. He nudged the boy next to him, cupped his hand, and said something to him. Greg was not supposed to hear it, and he didn't.

"Where was I?" Rocco continued, "Oh yeah, our names in lights - Rocco "The Rock" Hardknuckle vs. Gorilla-Face Greg Smith." All the onlookers cheered.

In an instant, he grabbed Greg around the neck and pretended he was going to throw him down. He began a rapid-fire chattering as an announcer would when calling a real fight. He said, "And The Rock has Gorilla-Face in a crushing headlock. Poor, weak Gorilla-Face is crying for mercy. C'mon new kid, cry for mercy like a good little boy."

Greg said nothing as he was led around in the circle, his head crunched securely under Rocco's armpit. Other students were now attracted to the scuffling and noise. And of course Rocco was always a popular drawing card. He was always one to watch if you wanted to see some action. Anytime Rocco had a headlock on some poor victim, onlookers were always quick to gather. Most of the kids were quietly watching. Some of the sixth graders, however, were urging them on.

One hollered, "C'mon Gorilla-Face, don't let him do that to you. Hang tough in there!"

Another shouted, "Grunt, Gorilla-Face grunt! It'll give you some extra power."

Greg was sizing up the situation as he was yanked this way and that. He didn't think Rocco was angry. That was good. Rocco for certain wanted to embarrass him. That was bad. Also bad, he noticed there was a solid line of kids circled around him now.

Rocco continued his chatter as his arm tightened around Greg's one and only neck. Rocco said, "All right Gorilla-Face, I'm giving you one more chance. Your last! You going to squeal for mercy or are you going to carry your ugly gorilla head home in your lunch sack?" Greg felt trapped. There were no good choices. He could give up and try to somehow make a joke out of it. He could try and get loose, but that could turn into a real fight. Besides, he couldn't beat Rocco if he had a baseball bat. *Nothing* he could do now would have a good outcome.

For reasons he did not quite understand himself, he chose to try and break free. He made a quick move. He put his hand on Rocco's elbow, and tried to slip his head out from under his arm. It didn't work.

The crowd, seeing Greg trying to break Rocco's grip, reacted noisily. They whooped, hollered and threw out comments to rally the two fighters. It was as if some foolish person tossed gasoline onto a fire. The crowd's reaction had the desired effect. The two opponents grappled with more emotion. Rocco no longer was smiling and he tightened his grip on Greg's head. Greg's ear was now bent over like the corner of an old playing card. And it hurt!

Then Greg hollered, "Rocco, Rocco, your fly is open!" Rocco was distracted enough where Greg could catch hold of Rocco's ankle. Greg pulled hard. Rocco's grip loosened as he tried to keep his balance. Legs are meant to go back and forth, not out like an arm. Some people are very acrobatic and can do the splits. Rocco was not an acrobat. To keep his balance, he had to let go of Greg's head completely. Now Greg was free and pulling the leg and Rocco was hopping around trying not to fall. Rocco managed to turn a bit so that his back was to Greg. His legs were no longer a wishbone ready to crack. Greg still held fiercely onto the ankle, keeping it as high as possible.

Rocco was no longer laughing. He was angry! His smile was replaced by an ugly scowl. He was kicking backwards hoping to free his leg. But without something to hold onto, he was always in danger of falling over with each kick.

The crowd was howling with laughter. With Rocco as mad as he was, Greg was afraid to let go. Greg was hoping the teacher on duty would come and break it up. He looked for her, but could not see through the human circle that had enclosed them. At this point, Rocco bent over and put both hands on the ground to give his body support, and then gave a mighty kick. Rocco's shoe came off and Greg could no longer hold on. The leg slipped free of his grasp.

Sounds of surprise were heard from the crowd and the kids quickly moved back to give the two more room. Greg knew the game was over now - this was a fight!

Rocco was up off the ground in a second. He hurled a round-house blow at Greg. Greg ducked and the blow glanced off the back of his shoulder and head. Greg grabbed Rocco's right arm just above the elbow and hung on with both of his arms. Rocco tried to get free to take another swing, but he could not.

Greg was scared and his knees felt like rubber. Rocco was able to turn enough to hit Greg in the back with his free hand. It was another glancing blow and it didn't hurt much. To avoid another blow, Greg let go of the arm and moved completely to the back of

Rocco and grabbed his waist. He thought if he could hang on and stay close, Rocco would be unable to face him. If he could not *face* him, he could not *hit* him.

Rocco wheeled around, but Greg hung tight to his waist and spun around with him. Then Rocco quickly changed direction and spun the other way. Greg had to squeeze harder to hang on. Greg's squeezing made it difficult for Rocco to take a deep breath. Rocco was trying to strike him with his elbow, but could not reach him. He suddenly bent forward trying to throw Greg over his back. This mighty lunge caused Greg's feet to leave the ground, but he still clung tightly to Rocco's waist. Once again, Rocco thrust his body forward. Greg's feet sailed off the ground even farther, but he still held fast to Rocco's waist. He began to feel like he was riding a wild bronco in a rodeo. Greg knew this was the only position in which Rocco could not hit him and he was determined to hang on no matter what. Next Rocco kicked behind him hoping to hit Greg's leg with his heel. He was successful several times, and the sharp blows hurt Greg's shins.

"*Where* is that teacher who is supposed to be on duty?" wondered Greg.

At the same time Rocco was kicking, he was also trying to undo Greg's grasp. Rocco was prying at Greg's fingers. He felt his fingers gradually slipping off one wrist. With a mighty effort, he was able to lock them again. But now Rocco was working on the fingers of the other hand. He knew it wouldn't be long before his hold would be broken and he would have to meet Rocco head on - face to face!

As Greg's grip loosened, he thrust his hands into Rocco's back pockets and hung on. Now Rocco had more room to move but he still couldn't turn completely around to face Greg. As Rocco struggled to free himself Greg heard a ripping sound. The seat of Rocco's pants had been repaired once and the seam had ripped loose a bit.

Greg was afraid Rocco would find enough room to get free. He decided it was all over. He could not hang on forever and Rocco would finally get loose and attack him. He figured he might as well get it over with.

Greg let go of one of the pockets and with his free hand gave Rocco a strong push in the middle of his back. With that push, and the fact that Rocco was already leaning forward, the entire seat of Rocco's pants ripped off. Rocco landed on his hands and knees. His rear end was covered with only a pair of raggy underpants that displayed more bare skin than cloth.

Greg stood there frozen in shock. He was holding the seat of Rocco's pants in front of him. It was a very funny scene. Everybody was howling with laughter. Some were holding their bellies and doubled over. One boy was rolling on the ground. Eyes watered from laughing fits. Some of the girls who were jumping rope ran over to see what all the commotion was about. They were just in time to see Rocco skidding on his hands and knees and his nearly bare buttocks in full display.

Girls cried in alarm, "Oh my goodness," and "Can you believe this!" Some girls covered their eyes but peeked through their fingers. Others covered their mouths in a gasp of absolute astonishment. Some girls were so embarrassed they *almost* didn't look.

Rocco got up but was clearly confused about what to do with his hands. Should be make them into fists and go pound on Greg? Or, should he use his hands to cover his very exposed backside?

Embarrassment quickly won out over anger. Rocco covered his rear with both hands and sprinted for the school door as everyone howled and pointed at the fleeing Rocco.

Chapter 25

The teacher on playground duty finally arrived. Her first words to Greg were, "You little bully! Why were you picking on that poor boy? You ought to be ashamed of yourself."

Miss Pennyworth was new to the school and was not aware of Rocco's reputation as *the* number one school bully. She grabbed Greg by the arm and roughly escorted him to the principal's office.

"Whatever is going on?" asked a puzzled Mr. Picklehoffer.

"This boy, uh, what's your name?"

"Greg, Greg Smith," he stammered.

"Yes," an angry Miss Pennyworth continued, "this boy, Greg Smith, *violently* threw another boy to the ground where he landed on his hands and knees. I heard the students refer to the unfortunate victim as "Rocco." And that's not all. In doing this hateful act, he tore out the entire seat of this poor lad's trousers. Look, see, the little monster is holding the evidence behind his back."

Looking daggers at Greg she demanded, "Now just show Mr. Picklehoffer what you've done."

Slowly, Greg brought the torn seat of Rocco's pants around and displayed them in front of the principal. Greg held the pants delicately with both hands, using only two fingers, and at an arm's length from his body. It was as if he expected some ugly bug to do a swan dive from the pants, to inside the neck of his shirt.

Hearing these words, Mr. Picklehoffer brought his hand to his chin and tilted his head to one side. He was obviously doing some deep thinking, trying to piece all this together. The only "Rocco" he knew was Rocco Hardknuckle. He was the one who had broken every school rule. He was the one who was the classic school bully. And finally, Rocco was the one student who regularly touched off his painfully pounding, migraine headaches.

Mr. Picklehoffer gazed at the ceiling and closed his eyes. In his mind, he pictured Rocco Hardknuckle sliding onto his hands and knees minus half his pants. A quiet smile spread over the principal's face. Miss Pennyworth looked puzzled.

Suddenly aware of his inappropriate smile, Mr. Picklehoffer quickly recovered from his blissful trance and said, "Thank you so much for being alert and breaking up this argument."

"Thank you Mr. Picklehoffer. If I hadn't been right on it, the situation could have turned into a *real* fight!"

Greg couldn't believe what he had heard. A real fight? This wasn't? He wondered if someone's teeth had to be laying on the ground before it's called a real fight? And what about the claim of her being, "right on it." In Greg's mind, overlooking this fight for most of the recess is *not* being "right on it." Give me a break, thought Greg. It *really* was, she being late for her duty and then not paying attention to what's going on once she got there. That's what it *was*. Also, Greg was angry at her for unjustly accusing him. But more was yet to come.

Mr. Picklehoffer said, "Thank you again, Miss Pennyworth, you may go back to your class and I will deal with this situation directly."

Miss Pennyworth turned to leave, but she stopped where Greg was now sitting in a chair by the door. She stooped down so she was eye level with Greg. Then she waggled her long boney finger in front of his nose and said angrily, "It's little brutes like you who grow up to start wars!"

Before the teacher could get out the door Mr. Picklehoffer cried, "Oh Miss Pennyworth, one more thing, where is Rocco?"

Miss Pennyworth replied, "The last time I saw that poor unfortunate darling he had escaped this little ruffian's grasp and was fleeing toward the school." With that, she shot one more glaring look at Greg, put her nose in the air, and marched out of the room.

"Excuse me, Greg," said Mr. Picklehoffer, "You sit right there. I'm going to scout around for Rocco."

The principal first looked to see if he showed up in the classroom. Rocco was not there. Then he checked the boys' restroom. He opened the door and called, "Rocco, are you in there?" There was only silence. Mr. Picklehoffer decided to go in and look just to be sure. There was a stall with the door closed. He walked to the door and knocked as he called, "Rocco, are you in there?" Seconds passed by with no answer. He knocked a second time only harder.

A quiet voice answered, "Yeah, I'm in here but ain't comin' out."

Mr. Picklehoffer decided to use humor to coax Rocco out. "Rocco," Mr. Picklehoffer said, "you've got to come out sometime. How will you eat? Do you expect us to slide a tray of food under the door at meal times? *And*, it's an awfully small place to sleep in. Plus, you'll miss Thanksgiving and Christmas." Mr. Picklehoffer waited several seconds for an answer. There was only silence.

In a somewhat pleading voice Mr. Picklehoffer said, "Rocco, what about basketball season. We'll need you on the team, not sitting in here on a toilet. How will you make baskets from that toilet? And play defense?"

No answer.

"Well," Mr. Picklehoffer said, "I'll just have to call your mother. Maybe she can bring another pair of pants for you and talk you off that toilet."

"Aw right, aw right, I'm coming out," he said in a tone suggesting defeat and surrender.

When he came out Mr. Picklehoffer said, "We keep some old clothes laying around just for emergencies such as this."

The principal walked around Rocco and looked him over. "Oh my! You are...uh, shall we say, *open* in the back," he exclaimed. "You stay here. I'll bring the pants to you."

Minutes later he returned with several pairs of pants on his arm. He said, "You try these on and wear the pair that fits you best."

The first two pair were so small he could not begin to squeeze into them. The last pair was very tight but he managed to barely wiggle into them. But the fit was not the only problem. Worse, was how the pants looked. These were the number one, ugliest pants he had ever seen. Red, white and blue stripes ran up and down the pant legs. He thought he probably looked like Uncle Sam. Rocco wondered if they were leftover from a Fourth of July parade.

When Mr. Picklehoffer came back into the room he looked Rocco over and held back a smile. "Well Rocco," Mr. Picklehoffer said, "they are a bit unusual but at least you're covered up. It's all we've got."

Rocco looked down at the pants that were a good five inches too short. He shook his head in frustration and pleaded, "I can't wear these ugly pants, Mr. Picklehoffer. I look like a circus clown or some character from a comic book. I just can't do it!"

Mr. Picklehoffer was trying to keep from exploding with laughter. He said, "I understand, Rocco. It's no problem. I'll just call your mother and she can bring you a pair of your own."

As Mr. Picklehoffer turned to leave, Rocco exclaimed, "No, no, don't call her." Then in a very low and disgusted voice he said, "I'll wear them."

"Well now, Rocco," Mr. Picklehoffer said, "I've got to go back to work. Can you promise me you'll go directly back to your classroom or must I accompany you?"

Rocco hung his head and muttered, "I'll go."

"I'll trust you to do that, so don't let me down," Mr. Picklehoffer said.

As Rocco got to his classroom door he had second thoughts about it. He said to himself, "No, I just can't go in there looking like some crazy clown. I *can't*, *won't*, do it!"

Then he remembered, he *promised* Mr. Picklehoffer he would return to class.

He stood there thinking about it and then made the decision. He was *not* going in.

But just at that moment, Scott and another one of Rocco's friends came around the corner. They had been on an errand for Miss Johnson.

Surprised, Scott asked, "Hey Rocco, where you been?"

The other boy stopped and inspected Rocco from head to toe. His gaze finally came to rest on Rocco's red, white and blue trousers. With an ever-widening smile, the boy simply said, "Nice pants."

Rocco had his faults but he did have a sense of humor. He also liked to be the center of attention. It was these two things that pushed him to reverse his decision, and enter the room. Entering the room was still a tough act but having two of his friends with him made it easier.

Scott opened the door and with a bow and a grand sweep of the arm said to Rocco, "After you." The students were busy working on a written assignment. As one student after another looked up to see who came in, there were muffled sounds of snickering. This soon gave way to outright laughter.

Comments began popping out from various parts of the room like sniper fire; "Circus in town?" "Uncle Sam?" "Where's your beard?" "Great ankles!"

Miss Johnson looked up to see Rocco. The sight of him in his too short, red, white and blue striped pants was too much for her to overcome. She shook her head, then covered her face with both hands to hide her laughter. She knew she must recover and get control of the class to save Rocco from further embarrassment.

She summoned up every ounce of self-control in her body, forced a serious expression on her face, looked straight at Rocco and - laughed out loud!

Recovering once more, and putting on her most serious face she said, "Rocco, I'm sorry. But you've got to admit those trousers *are* a bit too small for you. And the red, white and blue? Well, let's just say they're not your colors."

In the following seconds Rocco transformed himself. He no longer had that beaten dog look. He faced the class directly and confidently. Then he raised his arms over his head and made a "V" sign. He said, "I am Captain America," referring to a popular comic book hero of the day. Then in a loud, commanding voice he continued, "I have come to save the free world from those evil dictators who have attacked us."

He then promptly sat down and - split out the seat of his too-tight Uncle Sam pants. The ripping sound echoed throughout the now quiet classroom.

Miss Johnson did not interpret the ripping sound correctly. She frowned at Rocco and ordered him to excuse himself.

Rocco said loudly, "I will!"

Holding his geography book to cover his exposed backside, he stood up and faced the class. He raised a fist high in the air, and then said firmly, "Captain America must leave now. Keep the faith. I shall return!" Then lowering his voice said, "Mr. America needs to get some...uh...er...*reinforcements.*"

After the dramatic exit he went straight to Mr. Picklehoffer's office. Having had more than enough excitement for the day he appealed to Mr. Picklehoffer, "Would you *please* call my mother?"

When the secretary called Mrs. Hardknuckle she told her of the fight and Rocco's now two-piece pants. Upon arriving at the school, Mrs. Hardknuckle swept past the secretary without a word. She swung open the door to the principal's office without a knock and confronted Mr. Picklehoffer. Forcefully she wailed, "I should think that when I send my Rocco to this school, he should be safe. Whatever vicious hoodlum did this to my poor Rocco should be kicked out of school for good and locked up. Thugs like him are too dangerous to be free to walk the public streets."

Mr. Picklehoffer assured Mrs. Hardknuckle it would not happen again.

Before opening the door to leave she turned and faced him once more and shaking a finger at the principal said, "This is not the first time my Rocco has been bullied around in this school. Oh yes, he tells me how he's picked on here - all the time!"

Chapter 26

At dinner Greg told of his adventurous day at school. Mother said, "Maybe I'd better have a talk with Mr. Picklehoffer about your problems with Rocco."

Greg said, "No, I don't want you going to Mr. Picklehoffer. That would be embarrassing. It'd get around and everybody would think I'm kind of a sissy having you come in and all that."

"Well," Mother replied, "if I can help you in anyway let me know."

"How about moving back to Riverside?" Greg said. "That would solve all my problems."

As soon as his words were in the air he wanted to grab them and stuff them back into his mouth. Greg's mother put down her fork and looked at Greg. Then she closed her eyes for a few seconds and her face tensed up as though she were in pain. When she opened them tears ran down her cheeks. She attempted to wipe them away with the back of her hand which only smeared the liquid sadness over her face.

Grandma Henrietta offered her daughter a handkerchief. She took the little hanky, put her elbows on the table, and covered her eyes with both hands. Seconds ticked by. Grandma put her hand on her daughter's shoulder and gave her a gentle pat.

Mother then looked up at Greg. With reddened eyes and an

unsteady voice she said, "I'm so sorry. I just miss your father so terribly."

Then, as if an emotional dam had broken, a flood of tears appeared. Mother totally lost it. She cried uncontrollably as she pushed her chair away from the dinner table. Between sobs she breathlessly excused herself. As she hurried away she cried again, "I'm so sorry. I just miss him so much."

Greg could hear each quick step as she ascended the staircase. Each of those steps was like a nail driven into his heart.

Grandma Henrietta shook her head and said, "It's so sad. I feel so *sorry* for her." She continued on in a high shaky voice, "What a heartache she must be going through right now." And with tears welling up in her eyes, she excused herself, leaving her half-eaten dinner on the table.

Greg had never felt worse in his entire life. He wondered if Grandpa Henry would also have a meltdown and cry, and hurry away. How did that one dumb statement trigger so much grief, he wondered? Greg didn't know what to do. With his eyes cast downward, in a near whisper, he mumbled, "I guess I said the wrong thing."

Grandpa Henry pushed away his plate. He gently took Greg's arm and softly said, "It'll be all right, Son. You didn't know."

When Greg awakened the following morning he saw a note on his dresser. It read,

"Greg honey, I'm sorry about getting all upset last night. What you said should not have brought on my silly outburst. It was just that it reminded me of how happy we were in Riverside before this horrible war came to our doorstep. The war's not your fault. The truth is Son, it is *you* who keep me going. You help me more than you will ever know. Love, Mother."

Greg read the note. Now it was his turn.

Chapter 27

How would Rocco react at seeing him today? The question brewed in his mind constantly. After yesterday's humiliation, Rocco would have more reason to get revenge. Rocco was like a spring being wound tighter and tighter. With every turn the reaction would be more violent once set loose.

Cautiously, he left for school. He left early because he didn't want to meet Rocco on the way to school. Peering left and right and sometimes behind him, Greg hurried to school. He did not see Rocco on the playground. However, there were some early birds standing around talking. When they saw Greg they motioned him over.

"Hey if it isn't lucky ol' Clank Clunk Super Skunk," one boy hollered.

"Yeah, lucky to be alive!" another boy said.

"What you got planned for Rocco today?" somebody asked.

"Maybe you could tear up his shirt today," another suggested.

"No way, a shirt wouldn't be as good as the seat of another pair of pants," replied another.

They all laughed. Greg didn't know how to respond to all these comments. But all eyes were on him, expecting a response. He certainly didn't want to brag about it. The boy who said he was lucky had been right. And so that is exactly what Greg said, "Lucky? Right! I was *very* lucky."

One of the boys who so far had been quiet said, "I hope your luck holds up when Rocco comes on the playground. What'll you do?"

Greg shrugged his shoulders and said, "I don't know. Hope I can think of something."

Some of the boys were gazing off in the distance as if looking, or maybe hoping, Rocco would come. But Rocco was a no-show. He didn't show up on the playground. He did not show up late to the classroom.

After school began on the following day Rocco came in just minutes after the tardy bell rang. As he came through the door there was not the usual, confident swagger in his walk. He looked straight ahead and appeared very business like.

Greg was amazed at the change in the way Rocco acted. He looked and acted like a one hundred percent normal human being.

Miss Johnson often began the day by asking students if they had anything they would like to share about their lives.

Rocco raised his hand.

Miss Johnson said, "Yes Rocco, do you have something you'd like to share with the class?"

Rocco stood up and his eyes circled round the class and he said, "Well see, I got this beagle pup, Floppy. I already told some of the guys about him. Well see, I was going to train him. Shoot, *boy* was I going to train him! Well, I haven't been able to teach him one darn trick. Naw, not one!"

Rocco continued, "Like, I'll show him how to shake hands, then hold out a treat for him. He just sits there looking at me with those big sad eyes. He's either dumber than a wood post or smart enough to wait me out for the treat. Maybe he's training me more than I'm training him! Yeah, he just sits there a looking cute at me."

Then Rocco sat down and Miss Johnson said, "Thank you Rocco. Dogs are hard to train, especially beagles. Maybe you'll have to forget the tricks and love him just because he's yours."

Despite Rocco's new look, Greg was wary of what might happen at recess. As the hands of the clock marched toward 10:00, Greg tried to devise a plan that would keep Rocco away.

But two minutes before the bell rang, Miss Johnson said, "Rocco, I would like you to stay in and do the work you missed during your absence."

Saved, Greg thought, at least for now. Thankfully, lunch period was the same. Now all he had to do was to plan a way to get home safely. He needn't have. Two minutes before the bell Miss Johnson said, "Rocco and Greg, I need to talk to both of you after school."

After the class was dismissed, Miss Johnson told the boys each to get a chair from the table in the back of the room and bring it to her desk. Several students were in the hall hanging around the door near enough to listen. Miss Johnson asked, "Why are you still here? You're far too early for tomorrow's classes so scoot on home." They left.

Rocco had been walking rather stiff legged all day as though he couldn't bend his knees. When Rocco awkwardly hauled the chair to the desk, she asked, "Rocco, why are you walking so strangely? Can't you bend your knees?"

Rocco put on an exaggerated look of pain and said, "I have no skin left on my knees. Look, see." He pulled up a pant leg that revealed a badly skinned knee. A thin scab had formed that looked like it could break with a simple bend of the knee.

Miss Johnson exclaimed, "Why Rocco, that's a nasty scrape!"

"Yeah," Rocco replied, "Mom thinks I broke a kneecap. Maybe both of them." Then Rocco carefully lifted the other pant leg revealing an equally ugly scab. He said, "Skunk here...er... I mean Greg here, did that to me."

Miss Johnson raised her eyebrows and repeated the name, "Skunk? Is that what you call Greg?"

"Well," Rocco answered, "Yeah, we call him that now and then, but we don't mean nothin' by it. You know, just kidding around."

Miss Johnson paused as if she might be thinking about digging a little deeper into this "Skunk" issue. But then she thought it best to leave it for another time and stick with the issue at hand.

Miss Johnson asked each of them to tell their story of what happened. She asked, "Who would like to go first?" Neither Rocco nor Greg volunteered. "Okay, I guess I would like to hear your story first, Rocco," Miss Johnson said. "Oh yes! One other thing, I want no comment from you, Greg, until Rocco is done talking. Then you will get your turn. The same goes for Rocco when it is your turn, Greg."

It was clear to Greg that Miss Johnson had been through this many times before and probably with the same set of rules each time.

"Go ahead, Rocco," she said quietly.

"Well, this guy is always getting in my way," Rocco began. As he talked, he waved his arms and moved his head from side to side. "Everywhere I go, he is in my way and hassling me." Rocco continued, "I just got tired of it."

"Explain what you mean by hassling. Exactly what does he do?" Miss Johnson questioned.

"Well, it's hard to say," he answered. "He's just always there bugging me."

"If he is just *there*, and not doing anything to you, why should it bug you?" she asked.

Rocco said nothing. Neither did Miss Johnson. Greg thought the silence would last forever. Finally she asked Rocco, "Can you name *one* thing he has done to you?"

Rocco folded his arms in front of him and slumped further down in his chair. He looked sulky now as though he were pouting. He just stared out the window as if no one else was in the room.

Using the term lawyers and judges use in the courtroom, Miss Johnson asked, "Do you rest your case?"

"Yeah," he answered in a manner that bordered on rudeness, and then slumped another inch or two down in his chair.

"And what is your story, Greg?" asked Miss Johnson. "You know the old tale, it takes two to tango."

Greg squirmed in his chair. He finally got comfortable and began telling the whole story as he saw it. He began with the first day and how Rocco passed out the books, and ended with the recent fight on the playground.

She then turned to Rocco and asked, "Is all this true or do you think Greg is wrong on some points?"

"Well," said Rocco, "I really didn't want to get into a fight with him at recess but what else could I do? My friends practically said right out, that he's been making a fool out of me. I'm just not going to take that stuff."

"Rocco," Miss Johnson replied, "when Greg kicked the books over, what do you think he was trying to do?"

"Get me in trouble," Rocco answered quickly.

"Why might he want to get you in trouble?" Miss Johnson asked.

Rocco just sat there silently. Greg noticed that Rocco was now in trouble for answers.

Miss Johnson pressed again for his answer, "Why would he have reason to do that?"

Rocco just sat there, arms folded in a defensive position. Miss Johnson looked at him and waited for an answer. Greg felt uncomfortable with the silence, but the emptiness dragged on.

It was Rocco who finally gave in and broke the silence, "He was mad because I put his books on the floor. But I was just kidding around, that's all. And that's no reason to get all huffy and kick the books over and get me in trouble."

"Well, Rocco, remember that not everyone looks upon your actions the same way you do." Miss Johnson went on, "What might seem like kidding around to you, might appear to someone else as taunting, or worse, physically threatening. It might look that way especially to someone who is new to the school and doesn't know you. You must also remember that you *are* brought into the office for complaints like this more than most students. What I am hoping for is that your disagreements are over and you get on with the year without squabbling and fighting. Do you think that will be possible on your part, Rocco?"

After a long pause, Rocco finally replied, "I guess so." His statement lacked enthusiasm, but Greg figured it was the best Miss Johnson could hope for under the circumstances.

Then she turned to Greg. "What about you?" she asked.

"Sure," Greg replied. "I didn't ask to move here. I'd rather be back in Riverside right this minute, but here I am. I just want to get along and not be hassled."

"All right, it's agreed then," Miss Johnson said. "Let's just start the year all over again between you two. And one last thing. You've probably heard of the old phrase, 'Forgive and Forget.' Well 'forgiving' is not easy. And as far as 'forgetting' is concerned, not many people can ever actually forget the bad things that have been done to them. What the phrase means to me is to *act* as though it never happened, and just don't *ever* talk about it again. It's not easy but you'll feel better about yourself if you can do it."

Greg thought that was a bit much to ask, but he figured she had to end it some way. Greg knew he could never trust him and felt Rocco would always be out to get the best of him one way or the other. Rocco would never rest until he figured the score was even. He'd have a better chance of shooting baskets on Mars than to expect to start over again with Rocco.

Miss Johnson arose from her chair signaling this painful meeting was over.

Greg was relieved and happy Miss Johnson did not make them shake hands. But before he had a chance to enjoy the thought, she asked them to please shake hands!

This was really going to be hard. He noticed Rocco's eyes roll skyward. Rocco then blurted out the question, "Shake hands?"

Miss Johnson smiled as though she would enjoy this event. "Yes Rocco," she said, still smiling like an angel.

"Shake hands!" Rocco exclaimed again with a frown. Then his face screwed up and he shook his head vigorously back and forth like he had just swallowed a sour pickle.

Miss Johnson held her smile and tilting her head slightly toward him said, "Rocco, shaking hands is a common practice. I'm certain you've seen it done at some point in your lifetime. Might you need instructions?"

Rocco closed his eyes as if in deep thought. Then he opened his eyes wide and in a complete 180 degree turnabout, he said enthusiastically, "Oh Miss Johnson, that's a great idea, it would like - seal our friendship forever!" And with a quick move he arose from his chair and offered his hand to Greg. He said, "Put'er there Skunk. Oh...er...I mean Greg." He gave Miss Johnson a side glance hoping she would forgive the accidental slight."

Still sitting, Greg looked at Rocco's big beefy hand. He did not like this idea at all. Anything Rocco was *for*, couldn't be good. He sat back in his chair and pointed to Rocco's extended hand. He said to Miss Johnson, "To me, that thing looks more like a bear trap than a friendly hand."

Rocco pretended he was really hurt by Greg's comment. He put on his best pouty face, and turning to Miss Johnson said, "See, I offer him my hand of friendship and he doesn't trust me enough to take it. So much for friends forever huh!"

Greg, appealing to Miss Johnson said, "My right hand is the only one I've got and it's supposed to last me a lifetime."

Greg's concern about his "right hand that's supposed to last a lifetime," brought a smile to the face of Miss Johnson. Rocco thought it was funny also and grinned enough to show his big white teeth.

"Greg," Miss Johnson pleaded, "just give him your hand. If he squeezes you too hard he will never see another recess again this year."

Rocco's smile faded at the thought of no more recesses and he frowned at Miss Johnson.

Greg considered the deal. Maybe having his hand in a cast would be worth not having to see Rocco on the playground anymore. He took Rocco's hand. They shook and Rocco squeezed Greg's hand only hard enough for him to feel the bones of his knuckles rub together. It wasn't hard enough to complain, but hard enough to send a message.

"You may go now, Rocco, but I want to talk with Greg a few more minutes to see how he's getting along."

Rocco lifted himself out of his seat with a show of great effort and lumbered stiff legged to the door. "Good-bye, Rocco," Miss Johnson said.

Rocco's answer was some kind of sound that was between a mumble and a grunt that *could* have been "Good-bye." The answer bordered on discourtesy, but he evened things up by closing the door *very* gently, exactly as Miss Johnson had always told them to do.

Greg imagined she heaved a sigh of relief after Rocco left the room. Greg knew at least *he* felt that way. "Well," asked Miss Johnson, "other than the problem with Rocco, how have things been going here at Lincoln?"

"I'd rather be back in Riverside with all my friends," Greg replied.

"Sure, that's natural," she replied. "You'll have other problems too, but that's the way it is when you move," she said. "I moved when I was in third grade and the first day on the way home, two boys kept riding their bikes right at me. I'd have to jump out of the way at the last minute. I finally thought, that's it! I'm going to hold my own. I've got just as much right to be here as they have."

"When the next bike came at me, I didn't budge. Boy did I get smacked! The bike hit me straight on and knocked me flat. The blow knocked me down and I bruised my leg. I was sore for a week. But the show-off who hit me also fell. He hit his knee on the cement so hard he was still limping when I saw him the next day." Miss Johnson finally added, "Even though I got hurt, I am still glad I did it. I always tell this story to kids who move into our school and get hassled." Then she laughed, "I guess it wouldn't be much of a story if I had given in and continued to let them scare me off the sidewalk, now would it?"

"Well, Greg, you're excused now, but if you have any more problems about anything, just let me know. Maybe I can help. And always remember, time heals - just like skinned knees."

Greg gave her a "thanks" and a goodbye. It was difficult for Greg to think of Miss Johnson as being a skinny little kid in third grade. He thought it was nice of her to take some time and talk to him. As he walked home, he had a whole head full of things to think about.

Rocco was absent the following two days. Upon his return he ignored Greg for which Greg was thankful. Nobody mentioned the fight to Rocco. They knew better!

Chapter 28

The following week, Greg was occupied with going to school, homework, and his most favorite thing, shooting baskets. To Greg, shooting baskets was a form of art, like ballet, or modern dance. If your form looked good, the ball was more likely to go in. There was a full length mirror in the hallway of his grandparents' home. Every time he passed this mirror he would practice his shooting form. Did he follow through and extend his arm properly? Did his wrist and hand "fishtail" at the end of the shot? Were his feet positioned so that his body was balanced? Greg considered himself a "student" of the game and particularly of the shot. Like his coach in Riverside said, "Guys, we can run the plays and do everything else right. But in the end, if the ball doesn't go through the hoop we don't score. If we don't score we don't win. It's as simple as that. The ball *has* to go through the hoop!"

There was a basket hanging on a garage in the alley several homes down from the Olson residence. Greg went there often to practice his shot. The owners of the home didn't seem to mind kids playing there. In fact, one day the older man who lived there came out and shot a few baskets with him.

Friday morning Miss Johnson read an announcement from the office. It read: "All 5th and 6th grade boys who are interested in playing basketball this season should come to a meeting in the gym directly after school. Permission forms will be available."

The courts were crowded at recess as the announcement encouraged quite a few boys to practice. Since Greg was late getting out, he was waiting on the sidelines hoping to get into a game. Two boys came over and asked him if he wanted to challenge the winners and play with them.

"Sure," Greg said.

The two boys hollered for "winners," not only on the court where they were standing, but on the other court also. The trouble was that Rocco was playing on the other court. Greg hoped he would not have to play against him.

Unfortunately, it happened that Rocco's team had beaten their opponents first, so Greg and his partners were called to play them. As Greg and his group came onto the court Rocco, who had been taking a few practice shots turned and saw Greg. Rocco first looked surprised to see Greg. Then he bounced the ball hard on the blacktop with both hands. He stared at Greg and handed the ball to one of his teammates. He said, "My knees are starting to hurt. I'm going." and calmly walked off the court.

To Greg, it was obvious that it was not his hurting knees that caused Rocco to leave the game. It was the appearance of him, Greg, the one guy Rocco loved most to hate. That was the real reason he quit the game.

A replacement for Rocco was quickly found and play resumed. When the bell rang, one of the players said, "Let's meet after school and play."

Another said, "Good idea but let's meet at McKinley Park after dinner. It's a ways to go but the courts are better. We could probably play an hour or more before it gets dark."

McKinley Park was quite a distance, but Greg knew where it was. After dinner he jumped on his bike and started off. He rode to a point where he could see the courts. One court was being used but he was still too far away to recognize any of the players. As he drew nearer, he saw a player take a jump shot. It was Rocco! He could tell it was Rocco the way he shot the ball. Not many grade-schoolers could shoot a jump shot. His heart sank. Earlier today, Rocco walked off the court at the sight of him and he would probably do the same now. The other three guys, Scott, Alex and Phil were okay. Rocco was a different story.

He immediately turned his bike around and headed home. But then a second thought entered his mind. No, he would take a risk and hope Rocco would stay. He didn't even want to *think* about the worst thing that could happen.

As Greg rode up to the court, Rocco was the first to speak, "Doggone to heck, here comes my unlucky shadow. Every time I turn around, there he is, just waiting to get me in trouble."

"Skunk," Rocco bellowed at Greg, "GO HOME!"

From the other direction five guys walked onto the other end of the court. Three of them were as tall as Rocco. One of them hollered, "Hey look at this, the Lincoln 'Pussycats' are here." The others laughed.

These challenging words turned Rocco's attention away from Greg. Rocco eyed the five newcomers. What he saw was the starting five players from Madison School. It was the team that won the league last year, plus the end of the season tournament. They went undefeated and had beaten Lincoln twice last year.

Nobody from the Lincoln group responded to the "Pussycat" put-down. They were surprised and looked to each other, hoping someone could fire back an equally insulting response. Even Rocco was silent. But he quickly came alive and said, "Pussycats eh! Bring it on," and threw them the ball.

The tallest of the Madison group hollered back and said, "You only got four guys."

Another laughed and said, "Yeah and it'd take eight to beat us."

Scott said to his group, "We got Greg, that'd be five."

Rocco whined, "Oh man, I hate this," and gave Greg an up and down look of contempt.

Alex, another member of the Lincoln group pleaded, "C'mon Rocco, we've got to use him if we want to play."

Rocco grimaced and gritted his teeth as if in great pain. He turned to Greg who was still standing on the sidelines and said in a reluctant voice, "All right. C'mon Skunk. I can stand you, if you can stand me. But don't be screwing up, ya hear!"

They threw back Lincoln's ball and one of them hollered, "You guys bring it first. You'll need all the help you can get. Play to 12 by ones."

"Generous," Rocco yelled back.

The game began and was over very quickly. Lincoln lost by a good margin.

Each team stood around in their group. The Madison team was making plans for the next game. No one in the Lincoln group spoke. Nobody seemed to have an answer as to what to do.

Greg had been doing some thinking and finally made a suggestion, "They're a lot taller than we are but we're faster. Let's push the ball up the court really fast. See, *everybody* runs. We can get a shot off before their defense gets set. One other thing. If we get down there fast and still can't get a shot, we can run this play. Here it is. Rocco's man is taller than he is but Rocco is faster. So Rocco goes to the corner baseline and just waits there. We work the ball to the opposite side and then Rocco breaks for the basket. He'll be able to get around his man and get a pass for an easy lay up. Everybody stay out of the middle to clear it out for Rocco."

"Well," Scott said, "Can't do much worse. Let's give it a try."

The big tall lad who was guarding Rocco said, "You guys really want to play us again? You're sure suckers for punishment. Speaking for myself, I get more excitement out of swatting flies than playing you guys."

Another Madison player said, "Yeah, but flies bring a better game. They're smarter and quicker."

Another player said, "They're here, we're here, so were stuck with them. C'mon, let's get rolling. We need the practice."

Somebody else broke in with one more put-down, "Practice? You mean there was another team on the court? Didn't notice. Hope somebody shows up for the next one. We need the practice."

They all laughed.

Rocco was somehow able to sit on his anger. However, if a cartoonist were to draw him, black smoke would be rolling out Rocco's ears. The Madison player holding the ball at the other end of the court hollered to the Lincoln team, "Hey you, Lincoln Lunkheads, big time all-time losers, bring it to us," and rolled the ball to them.

On the first play, Phil passed the ball to Greg in the corner and Rocco waited in the opposite corner. As soon as Greg received the ball, Rocco made a break for the bucket. Greg led Rocco with a long bounce pass. The pass was perfect. Rocco got the ball two steps in front of the player guarding him. He went under the basket and made a nifty reverse lay up.

Madison took the ball down, but failed to score on their first possession. The next time down the court Rocco scored again, this time breaking in from the other side of the court. Again Madison failed to score when they lost the ball on an errant pass. Lincoln scored on a fast break this time with Scott getting a nice lead pass from Alex.

The Madison players were surprised at the speed with which the Lincoln players raced up the court. The player guarding Rocco simply could not keep up with him. On two occasions, Greg's man left him to double up on Rocco. Both times Rocco passed the ball back to Greg, who made a couple of long shots from the corner. At the end, Madison players were stunned to find themselves at the short end of a 12 to 5 score.

Alex gave Greg a lot of credit for the win. "Some game plan you gave us, Greg. Maybe we ought to sign you up for coach."

"Yeah," said Phil. "You watch, they'll want to go one more game for the best two out of three. What do we do next, coach?"

"Really guys," Greg answered, "they're big all right, but boy are they slow! They'll probably put someone else on Rocco, but that won't make any difference. I think if we don't blow our cool, and just stick to the same game plan we'll be okay. Just keep playing good defense and be *sure* to block out your man after each shot so they can't get in position for an offensive rebound. On offense, everybody get the ball out fast and beat them down the court. If we don't beat them on the break and have to set up, we'll go to Rocco just like before."

Greg looked to the opposite end of the court. From what he could hear, some of the Madison players were blaming others for the loss. The group did *not* look enthusiastic. The high spirited confidence they first displayed, appeared to have melted into the blacktop.

A Madison player hollered, "How 'bout one more? Best 2 out of 3?"

The Madison team's spirit lifted when one of their team members eagerly said, "C'mon, let's nail those guys this time, we can do it!"

But they could not. The Lincoln team did the same things they did previously, only better the second time around. Greg fed Rocco beautiful passes the whole game. Rocco responded by making over half the points. Several times, the Lincoln team beat Madison down the court for easy baskets.

The boys from Madison did not lose well. They blamed each other for taking bad shots. They blamed each other for loose defense. Only one player mentioned the superior play of the Lincoln team. He said to Scott as he left the court, "You guys are going to be tough this year, especially with that new kid. He knows how to set things up and he really moves the ball."

Greg overheard the comment and felt pleased that he was given some credit. Alex teased Rocco, "Hey, buddy, you're our big scorer out there today. Didn't know you could ever make two baskets in a row, let alone be the genuine, number-one high point man."

Rocco, who had been unusually quiet said, "It's easy when I get the ball that close to the basket. I got to admit that was one good game plan."

Rocco looked at Greg and said, "Got to change your name. Clank Clunk Super Skunk just doesn't fit anymore. You're clever like a fox. Yeah Fox, that's a good one."

Greg was pleased with his new name. Anything was better than Skunk. The name Fox was a step up from whatever else he expected. Greg did a quick review of all the events that had taken place between them - the game just played where they ripped Madison was the obvious highlight. Was there anything else that could, or would, help smooth their relationship? He wondered?

"Hey you guys," Rocco said, "Fox and I know this really neat spot that nobody else knows about. See, there's this big tree that fell down over a creek. You can walk out there on its side and watch the water go by and throw rocks at stuff. But I'll tell you straight out, you got to watch out for those man-eating turtles. Rocco turned and gave Greg a wink. Well, I was thinking, I got a lot of lumber from an old shed my dad and I tore down. I'll bet we could build a tree house up there before the snow flies. You know, like, have a hangout."

On the way home Alex and Rocco were talking about the team. Alex said, "Man, that felt good beating those Madison guys. That Greg, what are we calling him now? Fox, yeah Fox, he's a basketball brain isn't he."

Rocco remained silent for a moment and then said, "Truth is, I been doing some thinking and I guess maybe he knows about some other stuff too."

"What do you mean?" Alex asked.

"Hard to explain," Rocco replied. "To be honest with you, I haven't figured out yet myself. My mind's still chewing on it. But I'm getting there."

Then Rocco let out a long sigh, and with some hesitation said, "Just...well, see it's got something to do with my little beagle, Floppy getting run over by that car yesterday - and a turtle named Tubby."

With a heavy sigh, Rocco looked away and said no more. Alex asked no more. They walked home in thoughtful silence.

Chapter 29

In the days following the adventure with the Madison team, life became much easier for Greg. Rocco actually spoke to him three times with only one being a mild put-down.

When the basketball season started Lincoln got off to a great start winning their first five games. The coach was a teacher who really didn't know much about the game. He allowed the players to run things on their own. Greg, now known as the Fox, or just Fox, was always the one they turned to for direction and leadership.

The school gym had three rows of bleacher seats on one side of the court. Many students and some parents and teachers attended the games. Greg loved the crowd noise and enthusiastic support. Miss Johnson was always there cheering them on.

She told the class about her experience when visiting a cousin in another state. Her cousin played high school basketball under girls' rules. She explained, "There are six players on each team, three on defense and three on offense. No player can cross the center line." After drawing a diagram on the chalkboard she said, "It is like 2 half court, 3 on 3 games; 3 offensive players try to score on the 3 defensive players. If the offense scores, or if the defense gets the ball back, then the other side gets the ball and the game proceeds on the other end of the court. The players who had the ball previously get a chance to rest. My cousin played defense and said she would rather play offense so she could shoot the ball and score points."

One of the students asked, "Why are there separate rules for boys and girls?"

Miss Johnson replied, "They believe that girls aren't strong enough doing all that running the boys do." Several girls disagreed with this idea. Susie, the checker champ, was one of them.

Miss Johnson said, "Oh I agree with you and I believe someday girls *will* be playing the same as boys. I've always been a basketball fan. I dated one of the players on the team and he went on to play in college."

That evening at the dinner table Mother said, "Guess what? I have been assigned to another job. I'm now in training to become a riveter. And I'll tell you that rivet gun is not light. And noisy! My ears are still ringing. My arms are tired and my ears are ringing *but*, I got a raise. I'm now earning $1.05 an hour!"

Grandma Henrietta said, "Well that's nice Rose but remember to take good care of your health. If they ask you to do anything that's too stressful just tell them no."

"Mom," replied Rose, "If other women are doing this I guess I can too. I don't want the other workers to think I'm some kind of weakling."

Her mother replied, "Might be you'll have to make a choice about what's most important to you: your health, or your pride and money."

"Oh don't worry Mom, I'll be careful," her daughter replied.

To Greg, the conversation was a little weird. It was almost like a mother worrying about her little girl, but the little girl was a grown-up! He wondered whether he and Mother would have a similar talk when *he* was grown-up. Do mothers ever stop mothering?

Grandpa Henry asked, "Greg, how are you and old what's-his-name getting along? Any more funny stories? He's a character.

What's his name again?"

Greg replied, "Rocco, Rocco Hardknuckle. No. No funny stories. And yeah we're getting along a little better. And that's good. I'd rather be getting along with him than telling funny stories about him." Greg decided not to mention the game, and the details of how that helped. He still figured Rocco to be unpredictable. He would have to wait and see how things played out.

"Oh Greg," Grandma said, "I forgot. There's a letter for you that I laid on your bed. I see on the envelope it's from Mrs. Sutter's son, Steve. I remember you said you wrote to him. He was always such a nice boy."

Chapter 30

Greg could hardly wait to finish eating, excuse himself, and get upstairs to his letter. He bounced up the stairs two at a time. He grabbed the letter off his bed, tore it open and read it.

Part of the letter read;

"I was interested to hear you play basketball. Maybe we could shoot a few baskets when I get home. And speaking of home, I only have one more mission and I'm done here. After 30 missions I guess they figure you've done enough and they reassign you to a non-combat job. Of course I'm hoping for an assignment in the good old USA. Rumor has it our last mission is going to be a big one. I can't tell you much else about it, but I think I can tell you at least this much."

Greg could read no more. The next three lines in the letter had been censored. Instead of any writing, there were thick black lines. He held the letter up to the light hoping to make out some words through the blackness. There was nothing. What could be so secret that the censor would blacken it out?

This last raid was probably over by now. Greg's imagination was fired up by the mystery. Where did they strike? Was it one of those big raids where they send over 100 planes? Greg could not imagine 100 B-17s in the sky. Did Nazi fighter planes attack

Molly's Angel with all their guns a blazing? How many of the bombers made it through and got back to their base? And the big question, was Molly's Angel one of the lucky ones?

All these questions bounced around in Greg's mind. He looked at the letter again. Hidden under those thick, black lines were important words that must remain a mystery. Then an idea struck Greg that cheered him up. He would save the letter. When Capt. Sutter came home he could tell him what the so-secret words were that lie concealed under those heavy black lines.

Miss Johnson had encouraged the class to share their letter writing experience with the class. Each student could tell in which branch of the service their pen partners served. They could tell where they were stationed and find it on the wall map. If there was nothing of a personal nature in the letter, the student could even read the letter, or parts of it, to the class. Greg could hardly wait to bring the letter to school. His letter would be special because it had this big secret that had been censored.

The next day as Greg entered the hallway he did not see Miss Johnson standing in the doorway welcoming the students, as was her habit. In her place was Mr. Picklehoffer.

After the class was settled in, Mr. Picklehoffer explained, "Miss Johnson called in late this morning and said she would need a substitute today. We've not yet been able to find a sub on such short notice. But our school secretary, Miss Becker, is calling around now. It shouldn't be long before she finds one. In the meantime I will be your teacher."

Greg remembered Miss Johnson had been trying to shake a miserable cold. He figured the nasty cold germs had finally gotten the best of her.

When the class came in from recess both Mr. Picklehoffer and a sub were standing by the classroom door. When everyone was in and seated Mr. Picklehoffer introduced her as "Miss Snodgrass." He followed the introduction with a stern warning about what would happen if anyone misbehaved. He ended this lecture by looking directly at Rocco and saying, "We wouldn't want to miss any basketball games now, would we?" Greg hoped Rocco got the message.

He did not. Not two minutes after Mr. Picklehoffer left the room, Rocco launched into a coughing fit. It was the kind of forced coughing that sounded fake. Coming from Rocco, Greg *knew* it was fake. The entire class knew it was fake. The teacher, Miss Snodgrass, was 99 percent sure it was fake.

Rocco held one hand on his chest and held the other to his throat and gasped, "Please Miss *Snot*grass," emphasizing the 'Snot,' "I need to get a drink. I'm (cough, cough, cough) choking to death!"

Miss Snodgrass did not have to look at the seating chart to know the name of the "choking" student. She had been forewarned by Mr. Picklehoffer about Rocco and his devious, showboating ways. To Rocco, substitute teachers were prey and it was always open season. One time Rocco even made a sub cry. It made his day.

Miss Snodgrass looked down her nose at Rocco and said firmly, "Mr. Hardknuckle, my name is Miss *Snod*grass *not* Miss *Snot*grass."

Miss Snodgrass paused, as if wondering whether to allow Rocco to leave for a drink. While she thought about it, Rocco's face turned red as a beet, and he hammered on his desk with his fist, and gasped for air.

He ought to be in the movies thought Greg. Some of the students' faces turned from smiles to concern, however, so convincing was Rocco's performance. Miss Snodgrass finally thought it better to be accused of being permissive, than to have a student die at their desk. She could imagine what it would look like on her permanent record, or worse, on the front page of a newspaper.

"At the end of a school day, authorities extracted a cold corpse from a desk in the room where Miss Snodgrass was teaching. Earlier in the day the chocking student's request for water was denied by Miss Snodgrass."

No, not a good thing to have on a teacher's record *nor* in the headlines.

She gave in, "Yes Rocco. You may get a drink of water but come right back."

Immediately Rocco jumped out of his desk and stumbled toward the door still holding his throat. In between coughs he forced out, "Oh thank you Miss Snotgrass." As he opened the door, he turned his back to the teacher and gave the class a quick smile and a sly wink.

Minutes went by and Rocco did not come back. She looked out the door for him. There was no one at the water fountain and the hall was empty. She sat down and wrote a note to the office about the matter. As a student messenger was about to open the door to leave, Rocco entered.

When quizzed about his absence Rocco said, "Well, you see, I had this overdue book that I had to return to the library." Miss Snodgrass gave Rocco a short lecture about getting permission before going somewhere.

Rocco did not look at the teacher but instead he gazed around the room. He wanted to know if any of his "fans" were supporting him by giving him a smile. Some were.

Then, without even raising his hand he blurted out, "Miss Snotgrass, I've to go to the bathroom, okay?" He raised out of his desk assuming she would give him permission to leave.

He took not one full step toward the door before Miss Snodgrass sharply said, "No. Sit down!"

"But Miss *Snod*grass, I really really have to go!" he pleaded. Rocco emphasized the "d" in Snodgrass in hopes the show of renewed respect might earn his way out of the room.

It didn't work. Miss Snodgrass stared at Rocco for a moment and calmly said, "You should not have swallowed so much water."

When Rocco continued his begging she ignored him and turned to write a lesson on the chalkboard.

Scott, who sat directly behind Rocco whispered, "Rocco, just go in your pants. That'll sure get her attention."

Amy, the girl sitting next to Scott overhead his comment. Her picture of Rocco going in his pants was the funniest thing she had ever heard. She cupped her hand over her mouth to stifle a laugh. Ann, who sat across from Amy asked what was so funny. Amy told Ann. Ann told Jim. Jim told John. John told Marie. And so it spread across the class like a prairie fire on a windy day.

Miss Snodgrass had been writing on the board with her back turned to the class. She was unaware of the uprising until she heard the sudden explosion of laughter.

She had a super-serious scowl on her face and demanded, "All right, will somebody please tell me what's so funny?"

As so often happens, when a message travels through so many ears, the original message got twisted.

One of the last students to get the twisted message blurted out, "Rocco wet his pants!"

The class again erupted with laughter. Rocco was hollering, "Did not! Did not!" And with all this rumpus going on, the teacher was ringing the 'be quiet' bell and hollering at the class to - "Stop this laughing and settle down. NOW!"

When the class calmed down Miss Snodgrass looked at Rocco with great sympathy and said, "Rocco, I'm *so* sorry. Do you have a medical problem?"

At that moment Mr. Picklehoffer stepped through the door. "*Whatever* is going on here. I could hear this uproar in my office!"

Miss Snodgrass wrung her hands and with a distressed look said, "Oh Mr. Picklehoffer, I'm so glad you came in. Rocco here, has had an accident."

Rocco immediately began to explain the mistake but Mr. Pick-lehoffer would hear none of it. He raised his hands in a "stop" position, as if his hands were a wall that would prevent any of Rocco's words from getting through. He demanded, "Rocco, don't say one more word. Accidents like that can happen and it's terribly rude of your classmates to laugh. I would expect better of them."

The principal said in a voice filled with sympathy and understanding, "Please stand up Rocco, so I can see how bad it is."

Rocco jumped out of his desk and pleaded, "But Mr. Picklehoffer, there is nothing..."

Mr. Picklehoffer sharply interrupted Rocco again and insisted, "Rocco remember, not *one* more word. Accidents like this *do* happen sometimes. Please turn around and let me have a look at your front."

Rocco had given up on trying to say anything and just stood staring up at the ceiling with a look of anger, embarrassment, and complete hopelessness.

A puzzled expression crossed Mr. Picklehoffer's face and he exclaimed, "Why, I don't see a thing!"

Scott joked, "Maybe you better check out his backside."

Scott's suggestion brought the class from smiles to outright laughter again, as it was meant to do. Mr. Picklehoffer gave Scott a harsh look and commanded, "I'll see you in my office at lunchtime young man." He then looked over the class and said calmly, "If anyone has an explanation for all this I'd like to hear it." In a few minutes the pieces of this fiasco were sorted out and related to Mr. Picklehoffer.

The unsmiling principal left the room but not before glaring at Scott and with a stern reminder, "Remember - my office - lunchtime!"

Now, all was quiet in the classroom as if their pent up energy had finally spilled out and nothing more was left.

Miss Snodgrass was relieved. But this peaceful scene was broken by a quick movement. It was Rocco's hand. It went up. She saw the raised hand and immediately closed her eyes as if praying. After a few seconds passed, she recovered and in a tired, but most polite voice asked, "Yes Rocco, may I help you?"

Rocco, in a very serious and courteous manner asked, "I was wondering Miss *Snod-d-d*grass," emphasizing the 'd' sound so firmly it became another syllable, "if I could use the bathroom now?"

At this point, Miss Snodgrass felt like a raccoon that had been flattened by the 18 wheels of a semi-truck. In a weary, but extra polite voice, she answered, "Why yes Rocco, of course you may go." Secretly, she said to herself, "Go on the moon if you want to. But please, please, just don't come back here!"

Chapter 31

When Greg returned home after basketball practice he noticed several cars in front of Mrs. Sutter's house. Upon entering his house he saw his Grandpa, Grandma and Mother sitting in the living room looking very sad.

"What's going on," Greg asked. "Something bad happen?"

"Yes," Mother said. "Mrs. Sutter received a telegram very early in the morning." Mother then paused to steady her breathing. "Greg, her son is missing in action."

"It's such a pity," Grandma Henrietta said. "He was *such* a nice lad and he was so close to making it."

Greg was stunned. He felt like he actually *knew* Capt. Sutter. He sat down, tears welling up in his eyes. He wiped his eyes with his forearm as his mother came over and put a hand on his shoulder. She said, "Greg, I'm so sorry."

He said softly, "I'm going to my room." Greg had hung his B-17 Flying Fortress model on a string from the ceiling above his bed. Days before he had carefully changed the name of the plane. Below the window of the cockpit was now printed "Molly's Angel."

For several seconds he stared at the B-17 he had so patiently constructed. Suddenly, he yanked the model from the string and with both hands, slammed it to the floor. As he viewed the debris, his tears distorted the shapes of the many pieces of the B-17 that lie at his feet.

Greg allowed his body to fall limply onto the bed. He recalled the newsreels showing the life and death battle between the U.S. bombers and the Nazi fighter planes. Before, he had always focused on the Flying Fortresses with their machine guns spraying their lethal lead at their attackers. And what a thrill it was when one of the Nazi fighters was hit and set ablaze. Smoke would billow out from the aircraft and it would spin out of control and crash into the ground.

Now, he was forced to imagine the other side of the coin. What bad things happened to the Nazi fighters could as well happen to the U.S. bombers. Molly's Angel could have been the plane hit, smoking, and tumbling out of the air, to smash into the ground.

Greg knew this was always a possibility. However, this picture was always hidden somewhere in the dark corners of his mind. But with Capt. Sutter now MIA, it came racing, unwanted, into his awareness. For Greg, the picture of this war suddenly changed from some glorious adventure to a personal tragedy.

And then he thought of his father. Would he ever see him again?

It was a quiet breakfast the following morning. Mother had come to his room last evening to see how he was doing. They talked briefly about the sad event. She said some hopeful words to him and this made him feel only a little better. His mother noticed the airplane parts that littered the floor but said nothing. She knew the message that lay in the shadows behind this act...and she agreed.

Earlier in the morning before going to work Mother left a note at his place at the table. It read;

Greg Dear, I hope you're feeling better this morning. Remember two things; there is always hope, and time heals. There's going to be some tragedy in all of our lives. Each of us must find our own way through it. Last, I know I've said this before son, but I feel I must say it again. Know that I will always be there to help you in whatever way I can. Love, Mother.

Entering the playground Greg just wanted to be alone. He found a spot by the building that was reasonably quiet and out of the way. Within a minute however, Scott ran over to him and said, "Hey, what's the matter guy? You look just awful. What in the heck's wrong?"

Greg unloaded the whole story on Scott: Mrs. Sutter, the bike, the picture, the letter, everything. Scott listened patiently. "Well," Scott said, "missing in action doesn't mean he's dead. I'm real sorry. I guess you just have to hope for the best. I've got to run now and see Rocco about some stuff."

Miss Snodgrass was again waiting at the door to greet them. It was an orderly start for the day. Even Rocco entered the room without his usual wild-man flair.

Miss Snodgrass began the class by asking them the question; "Do you kids realize the importance of the times we're living in? This period in history will never be forgotten." She talked about the "Home Front" and all the ways it was different from normal times. She listed victory gardens, rationing of food and other scarce items, scrap drives, and the sale of U.S. Savings Bonds used to help pay for the war. Last and most important she said, "Winning the war is vital. If we didn't win the war we would be ruled by other nations and then we would lose our freedom." Greg thought that was really scary. He could not imagine what life would be like being ruled by another nation. Once more he wondered if the war would last long enough where he would have to put on a uniform and join the battle.

During the art class the students were milling about working on their project. Greg needed to use a stapler but it was empty.

"Miss Snodgrass," Greg asked, "Can I get some staples out of your desk? I know where they are."

"Yes Greg, you may," she replied.

He went to the drawer of the desk where the staples were kept. As he was about to open the drawer he noticed for the first time, a small framed picture. He picked it up for a closer look. It was of a uniformed officer with silver wings pinned to the breast of his jacket. He was amazed to see how closely it resembled the picture in Mrs. Sutter's home. Turning the picture for better lighting, he was now certain it was Capt. Sutter. Then, he noticed the writing in the bottom corner; "To Pat, with Love, Steve."

Greg had never been more surprised by anything in his entire life. He just stood there, stunned by what he had discovered. Another, closer look confirmed it. Yes, this *was* Capt. Steve Sutter, the bomber pilot to whom he had written, and whose return letter was in his pocket. It was the same pilot whose bike he had ridden to school that very day. Yes, it was the same young officer who now might never see his home, his mother, nor his love, Pat Johnson again.

The pieces of this puzzle suddenly locked into place; their childhood connection, seeing Miss Johnson at Mrs. Sutter's house, and now, Miss Johnson's absence at the same time of the notice about Capt. Sutter. It all came together - but tragically.

He sat down in the teacher's chair and laid the picture in front of him. With his elbows on the desk, he cupped his hands over his eyes to hide the tears.

After a moment Greg felt a hand on his shoulder. He looked around to see Rocco. Rocco said, "Scott told me the story about how you got your bike and you writing to that pilot and all." And then, pointing to the picture, Rocco said, "But jeez Fox, we didn't know it was *him!*" He gave Greg's shoulder a caring squeeze, and said, "Fox, you must be hurtin' something terrible right now. I'm just *real* sorry."

Epilogue

INTRODUCTION TO THE EPILOGUE

There are fables that tell of ancient crystal balls that have the mysterious ability to foretell the future. This author was thinking it would be great to find one of those future-telling ancient crystal balls. Just maybe we could peek inside it and see what happens next to our beloved characters.

I've heard tell of these aged crystal balls being found in spooky attics of old houses. I own a house that's over a hundred years old. Maybe I'll just climb up into my spooky attic and see what I can find.

I hack through dense entanglements of cobwebs in the dusty corners of my century old attic to see what I can find. Lo and behold, what is this? Ah ha! I find a very dusty old crystal ball!

I gently wipe the glass clean and turn out the light. (I've heard tell the future comes "to light" better in the dark.) But first a warning: a crystal ball never exposes an entire lifetime - only a peek - a scene or two. It's up to your imagination to take a scene revealed inside the crystal ball and to run with it! So dust off your imagination and come with me for a walk into the future. With luck, maybe we can view the different roads on which our friends will travel.

Are you ready?

EPILOGUE
Captain Steven Sutter

As I peer into the crystal ball, I see Capt. Sutter with both hands on the controls of his bomber, Molly's Angel. The shuddering, limping plane has been ripped by flack from the antiaircraft fire below. Number 3 engine sputters to a stop and the prop now stands as motionless as a soldier snapping to attention. Black smoke streams from the crippled engine and traces of flame can be seen darting through the rolling blackness.

Capt. Sutter whispers in a tight voice, "C'mon Molly old girl, fly on. Bring us home." But his chances of nursing this pounded plane back to England is fading in step with the ever slowing speed of the aircraft. The horrific flack is the worst he has ever experienced. The hailstorm of shells has blown through the plane's thin aluminum panels without letup.

His copilot and good friend lie slumped on his side. There is nothing he can do for him. It is all Capt. Sutter can do to fight the stubborn controls to keep the craft on course. He has to focus on the 150 switches, gauges, dials, cranks and handles to keep this wounded bird airborne. He can detect no signs of life from the navigator, bombardier nor crew chief, all of whose stations are near him. Since the radio is dead he knows nothing about the condition of the others in the 10 man crew. Molly's Angel had dropped out of the formation long ago and now flies alone in the night sky.

Most of the crew members have been together for all 30 missions, this one being the last. To a man, they consider Molly's Angel a very lucky plane. Also in their minds, there is no better pilot in the 8th Air Force than Capt. Steve Sutter. Many times against all odds, he has delivered them back to their home base. But this day is the worst.

The bursting of shells gradually stops. He is out of range of their relentless fire. But now he senses he is no longer alone in the night sky. He is correct. Looking around he spies two Nazi fighter planes above and to the right of him. They are like sinister shadows barely visible in the darkness. They were likely sent up to search for any straggling, wounded bombers that have not yet escaped back to England.

In the animal world it would be like a lion stalking a herd of antelopes. A hungry lion will wait for an antelope so sick or weakened it can no longer keep up with the herd. This is a common strategy used by all predators. Now the predators are the two Nazi fighter planes. Molly's Angel is the weak and wounded prey.

"Where is our gunfire?" he wondered. The silent weapons tells him either his guns, or his gunners, are disabled.

The lead fighter plane suddenly bursts forward and races far ahead and out of sight. Capt. Sutter knows what is coming next.

The most vulnerable part of the B-17 is the nose and that is exactly where the German fighter planes had learned to attack. The fighter makes a long, round turn and heads straight for the nose of the B-17. It is charging in for the kill. The two planes come speeding at each other like two trains on the same track. Tracer bullets from the fighter light up the night sky and scream in on Molly's Angel.

There is an ear shattering blast. Then all is silent. Capt. Sutter's body slowly twists, turns and falls through an empty sky. As he comes out of this dream-like trance and back into consciousness, he is slow to realize what is happening to him. It is an eerie, out-of-this-world feeling.

In seconds though, the cold, biting wind beating on his face brings him back to his senses. But how did he get here he wondered? Was he blown out of the aircraft? Did he jump? He remembers nothing after the ear-splitting blast that yet pounds in his brain.

He knows the plane was beyond the coastline and he is now falling over the North Sea. What to do? He can think of only two terrible options. The first is pulling the cord on his chute and to sail into the freezing waters of the North Sea and die a torturous death by drowning. The second is *not* pulling the cord and to allow himself to free fall onto the surface of the water. There he will die upon impact when slamming into the water's surface. Both options were a grim choice of how to die. He made the decision. He will get his death over with quickly. He will *not* open the chute.

His last thoughts are of the two loves of his life, Patricia Johnson, and his mother Molly. Upon thinking of these two grand women to whom he is saying goodbye, he *cannot* do it. He will seize upon whatever sliver of hope is left, to be with them once more. Frantically he fumbles to find the pull ring of the chute and pulls it hard!

The chute opens and billows above him. He feels the abrupt pull of the harness as the chute fills with air and checks the momentum of the free fall. He can see nothing below. It is as if he is falling into a black hole. He braces himself for when he will plunge into his cold watery grave.

Only seconds later, Capt. Sutter's body hits, not with a splash, but with a crashing thud! Yes, he is in the North Sea, but on a small island in the North Sea. Had he landed a bit east or west from this point, he would be gasping for his last breath of air before being dragged to the bottom of the frigid, salty waters.

He cannot think about his good fortune because of the gripping pain in his left leg. He remembers the first thing an airman is supposed to do is to bury the parachute. But he cannot stand, let alone bury the chute.

Next he hears loud shouting in German, and fast footsteps beating through the dense brush. Seconds later, two German soldiers break through the heavy thicket of underbrush with their guns ready for action.

For Capt. Steve Sutter, this is the beginning of a long period of imprisonment. For almost three years he endures hunger and hardships in a series of German POW camps.

EPILOGUE
Sergeant William "Will" Smith

Greg's father, Will Smith, is sent to England for more training. All the countries on the continent of Europe have been overrun by Nazi Germany, except for Russia. Russia, also known at the time as the Union of Soviet Socialist Republics (USSR), is a very large country Germany has not yet conquered.

Being an island, England is difficult for Germany to attack. It is separated from the continent of Europe by a narrow strip of ocean called the English Channel. It is in England where the Allies are secretly training their soldiers to invade Europe. The term "Allies" means all those nations who had teamed up to fight Hitler's Germany and Italy's Mussolini. The Allies include U.S., Canada, England and many other nations. Their mission is to cross the English Channel and take the Nazis by surprise.

D-Day is a military term for when a big important battle is planned to begin. The Allies plan D-Day for June 6, 1944 when 150,000 soldiers on 6,400 ships and landing craft will cross the English Channel to battle the German army. Sergeant Will Smith will be one of those 150,000 troops. At dawn, Sgt. Smith finds himself on a large troop ship about to go into battle. The ship anchors far from the land because the water is too shallow for a large ship to reach shore.

Webbing that serves as rope ladders for the soldiers is dropped from the sides of the ship. Sgt. Smith climbs down this webbing where many small landing craft are bobbing in the water, waiting for the soldiers. The weather is terrible and the water is choppy with strong high waves. As he looks down the side of this huge ship he can see the soldiers are having trouble getting into the smaller craft. Some of the men have fallen into the water.

When he reaches the bottom of the webbed ladder he tries to time his step when the ever-moving craft is closest to the side of the ship. He makes it! The next man who follows him, however, takes a bad spill and hits hard on the side of the landing craft.

When there are about 25 men in the boat the driver revs up the engine and it speeds away from the transport ship. The small craft pitches dangerously in all directions. The troops hang on to prevent being thrown from the boat. After a few minutes, several of the men become seasick and throw up. Sgt. Smith feels queasy but manages to keep his breakfast down where it belongs.

Soon artillery shells begin landing around them. One of the boats close by is hit and the soldiers are hurled into the sea. When they are approximately 25 or 30 yards from shore, the craft stops abruptly throwing the troops forward. They have run upon a sandbar and are stuck. The troops begin jumping off the boat and into the cold ocean water. They find themselves in water chest high. Holding their guns high overhead, they trudge toward the shore. Sgt. Smith watches several of the men go under. He thought they most likely stepped into a drop off. Although several waves splash over his head, he manages to keep his balance and wade to shore. His water soaked body and back pack become extremely heavy. He looks back to see another boat blow up either from hitting a mine or by being struck by an artillery shell. Another boat overturns in the rough water.

Of all the troops in the first assault, only about one out of every three soldiers actually makes it to shore. Sgt. Smith is one of the first to land. The beach was nearly empty when he first sets foot on the shoreline. But now it is crowded with other soldiers. In front of them rises a high cliff where German soldiers are firing down on them. The German unit is the very tough and experienced 352nd Infantry unit.

The American soldiers lie in the sand trying to avoid the hail of bullets coming at them from above. The Allies had given names to the five beaches where they were attacking. The beach where Greg's father had landed was called Omaha Beach. Of all the beaches, Omaha is the best defended.

He had been promoted to Sergeant, owing to his leadership skills and good judgment. And so it is, on D-Day June 6, 1944, Sergeant Will Smith, of the 1st Battalion, 116th Infantry, is in the first wave of troops to hit the shores of Omaha Beach.

Those troops lucky enough to make it to shore lie prone, staying low in order to avoid being hit by bullets whistling all about them.

Greg's father lie watching bits of dirt and sand fly up as bullets hit the beach close by. For a moment, Sgt. Smith is able to shut out the noise of war. He is certain that death will soon overtake him. He closes his eyes and whispers a quiet goodbye to his wife Rose and to his son Greg.

In the moments that follow, he makes a decision. If death is a certainty, he is determined *not* to be shot cowering on his belly with his face in the sand. Sgt. Will Smith struggles to his feet. He calmly stands tall and looks back over his shoulder. With a long sweep of his arm he rallies the troops to press forward into the withering fire. Seeing this act of courage, other groups of soldiers follow his lead and charge toward the towering cliffs.

At the end of the day, all five beaches are taken by the Allied forces. Omaha Beach is by far the bloodiest battle. There are over 2,000 casualties, that is soldiers either killed or wounded. Afterwards it is called "Bloody Omaha." Sgt. Will Smith survives. He also survives many other battles, including the famous "Battle of the Bulge."

After months of fighting, Germany finally surrenders. (Italy had surrendered months before this.) May 8, 1945 is called "V-E Day" which stands for victory in Europe.

Can you imagine how happy Greg and his mother are to see Father again after an absence of almost three years? It is estimated 183,000 children lost their fathers during WWII. Greg is *not* one of them.

EPILOGUE
Miss Patricia Johnson

Who is this we see in the cockpit of a P-38 fighter plane? Look closely. Why it's our teacher Miss Patricia Johnson!

She is taking this P-38 straight up, thousands of feet into the atmosphere. Now she puts the aircraft into a graceful loop and plummets straight down toward the earth at a near record breaking speed. The wings and fuselage seem to groan under the stress.

Not to worry though, at the last second she pulls out of the deadly dive and heads back up into the clouds.

Whatever could this scene be about?

After Miss Johnson learns Capt. Sutter is missing in action she wants to become more active in the war effort. Teaching is certainly important, but she wants more action.

She decides to join the WASPS. WASPS is an acronym for Women's Air Force Service Pilots. The purpose of this organization is to have women fly non-combat missions. The male pilots can then be sent to fly combat missions in the war zones.

These women pilots fly all sorts of missions, mainly in the U.S. New planes have to be flown from the factories where they are built, to airbases. Aircraft have to be flown to facilities to be repaired. Some women fly planes that tow targets behind them. A very few of the best become test pilots. They fly newly developed aircraft to see if they meet safety and performance standards.

Pat Johnson had learned how to fly when she was a teenager in high school. Her uncle Fred owned a plane, did crop dusting and gave flying lessons. He taught Miss Johnson's three cousins to fly, and at the same time offered his niece an opportunity to learn also.

She was a quick learner. Uncle Fred said, "Pat, I have never had a more apt, quick thinking student than you."

At the end of the school year she resigns her teaching position and applies to join the WASPS. She is accepted and completes a rigorous training program. Trainees must learn to fly all the military aircraft from small fighter planes to large bombers.

After a few months of routine flying missions she is rated one of the best pilots in the WASPS. Because of her superior flying skills she is offered a test pilot's assignment.

Being a test pilot is very risky. Aircraft designers never know for sure how their new aircraft will perform until it actually goes airborne. It is a test pilot's job to find out. They put the plane through stressful maneuvers. Test pilots discover how a plane holds up in a tight curve, or in a dive. They must have a good understanding of aircraft, and be able to think quickly if things go wrong.

Pat Johnson is aware of all these dangers. But she feels the need for excitement to help distract her thoughts from the constant worry over the fate of her fiance Capt. Sutter.

And so it is, our sixth grade teacher Miss Patricia Johnson, becomes one of the most reliable test pilots in the Women's Air Force Service Pilots organization.

EPILOGUE
Greg's Mother Rose

Greg's mother keeps her job as a riveter at the defense plant for the remainder of the war. Rose and some other women at the factory have their pictures taken by a photographer from the government. The U.S. government wants to encourage more women to work in defense plants like the Happy Toy Co. These pictures show the nation a woman can work in a factory and still be charming and attractive. They want the public to realize that just because you happen to be a female factory worker, doesn't mean you are some-how less of a woman. Well, Greg's mother, Rose, *is* charming and attractive.

Not too long after the photos are taken, posters appear show-ing a pretty female factory worker with her sleeves rolled up and making a muscle with her right arm. It is displayed nationwide and becomes one of the most famous of all WWII posters. It is called "Rosie the Riveter." Greg wonders whether his mother's photo might be the inspiration for this poster!

Every time Greg sees the poster he feels very proud of his mother. In large print the caption reads, "We Can Do It!" Each time he reads the words he is reminded of what his mother said to him when he questioned her decision to go work in a defense plant. It was this; "Listen to me Greg. I can do anything anybody else can do. I will do this for my family - and for my country." She meant it. She did it. Greg never once forgot those inspiring words.

EPILOGUE
Final Scene

The lighting in the crystal ball is growing dim. It appears as though any further clues must depend more upon our imagination than from within this dusty old crystal ball.

But wait! Another foggy image is coming into focus. I see a sign that reads "Las Vegas." Now I see a large audience and they are rolling in the aisle with laughter.

There is a very attractive couple sitting in the front row. I notice them because it looks like Greg and Sue, the checker champ, all grown-up. Their image is not clear enough to be certain. Probably not. Besides, what would they be doing here anyway?

On stage is a large, confident fellow obviously telling jokes. It appears as though he's a standup comic and he's knocking their socks off with his funny lines. He paces back and forth and carries a microphone in one hand while waving his other arm around in the air. He seems to be talking with his whole body.

Whatever does all this mean? I can't imagine! Can you?

The End

About the Author

Harvey Erikson is a retired teacher having taught 36 years in elementary and middle schools. His writing draws from observations and experiences from his long career in education.

This is his first novel.